Cat and Mouse

A.M. Offenwanger

AMOVITAM PRESS

amovitam press

Also by A.M. Offenwanger

Contents

PROLOGUE

"ARE YOU CERTAIN OF this?" the deep voice demanded harshly. Thick candles guttered in their massive carved holders, outlining the silhouette of a heavyset man facing into the room. A slight figure appeared from the shadows, bowing deeply.

"Yes, my lord." Another bow. "The black traitors have obtained the scroll and cast the portent, and received word of the power of the slave. They seek him. But as yet they know not his name nor dwelling, and..."

A heavy fist struck the table.

"He must be removed!"

"Yes, my lord." The pale face took on a sly look. "Your humble servant has news to this end, good news, my lord, which your humble servant found at great cost to himself."

"Well?" The powerful shoulders shifted under the gold-embroidered cloak.

"A portal has opened, my lord, a gate that was closed for many a hundredyears, to a land we could not enter. My lord might send the slave thence, bound thrice. The seer gives assurance that there are stones left in the treasury, the blue stones which might take a man across..."

"Ah! Very well. See that it is done." A coin glittered briefly in the candlelight. "If word of this reaches outside these walls, you will regret it. Go!"

"Yes, my lord!" The slight figure bowed deeply and withdrew into the shadows.

A shimmering vortex of blue light forms in the middle of the moonlit quarry, reflecting turquoise off the steep rock walls, whirling, spinning. Two figures appear, staggering, in its centre. The circling light slows and dissipates as the dark outlines resolve themselves into a man gripping the arm of a young boy. The man steadies himself, pushes the boy away, casts a glance around him, then strides out through the entrance of the quarry onto the plains. Silently, the boy clambers to his feet and stumbles after the man toward the sleeping city's dim lights shining on the horizon.

CHAPTER 1

E NOUGH WAS ENOUGH. CATRIONA picked up the baby, yanked open the door to her new husband's workshop, marched in, and deposited the little girl at her father's feet.

"She's all yours!" she said. "I'm going out, I need some air!"

She snatched Guy's cloak from the hook behind the door and stomped out into the clearing that surrounded the cottage.

One day—they had been married just one day. And actually, had only known each other for five. What on earth had she been thinking? Already Cat was so frustrated with the man she could scream. She hadn't—screamed, that is—because she didn't want to scare her new little stepdaughter. Bibby didn't deserve to be caught in the middle of yet another marital fracas; she'd had enough of that with her birth mother.

But Cat needed to get out of that cramped one-room forest cottage and let off some steam. She turned left and marched along the path that led past the clay pit. Five days of never having a moment to herself (the draughty outhouse at the back of the cottage didn't count); five days of trying to cope with being thrown into a totally new world with new rules where everything was different; five days of living in conditions almost as primitive as on a camping trip back in America—or even more so, if you went camping in an RV with hookups and running water. Which Guy's place definitely didn't have.

And that's what had sparked the big argument.

Guy's aunt, the formidable and no-nonsense Ouska, had amenities at her house. Oh, no electricity or central heating, of course. But she had indoor plumbing of sorts (run by a hand-operated pump, but still, it was inside the house), and she had a hot water tank over the cook stove that delivered lovely warm water to her bathroom behind the kitchen. Her *indoor* bathroom.

Guy's cottage, on the other hand—her own cottage now, Cat reminded herself—had nothing much more than four walls, an open fireplace, and a cold-water pump on the outside of the pottery workshop.

So Cat had asked Guy whether they couldn't have one of those hot water tanks in the cottage, too. That was *all* she had asked! And he got a look on his face like she'd requested gold plating on the door knobs, had huffed air out his nose and muttered something about "expensive" and "difficult", and finally said the cottage was what it was and that was that. And then he'd turned on his heel and vanished into his infernal workshop to presumably make more of his infernal pottery, leaving Cat alone, literally holding the baby. *His* baby.

Leaving her alone. Cat sniffed. That was the real issue, wasn't it. Just like last night. They had been married, yesterday, by the peculiar little private ceremony of this world—they had spoken the words of marriage to each other, and he had given her the silver necklace that served for a wedding ring in this place. Cat reached up to her neckline and fingered the filigree cat pendant at her throat. It meant they were married, didn't it? Or had she misunderstood that?

Yesterday, they were so happy... Come nightfall, they had tucked up the baby on the little pallet in the corner of the room. And then Guy—Cat sniffed again—Guy had given her a lingering kiss... and then taken a bed roll and gone to sleep by himself on the floor of his workshop!

Was that another peculiar custom of this world? What did they mean by "married", if it wasn't—well, sharing the bed? She could have sworn Guy was attracted to her "that way", that she wasn't the only one who had sparks shooting up her arm when they accidentally brushed each other—let alone those kisses...

Cat turned off the forest path into the small clearing where she had first arrived in this world. The Arbour, they called it. The blue bark of the Septimus Tree winked at her from between the screening branches on the right. She found a convenient, large rock and sank down on it, burying her face in her hands. What had she got herself into? What had come over her?

Yesterday, she had been so sure that it was the right thing for her to stay in this world, that this was the place for her to be. Well, actually, she was still sure of it. It just seemed right, she had no doubt about it. Being here was right; being with Guy and little Bibby was right.

But why was Guy so—so—difficult? She knew practically nothing about him. On rational consideration, it had been colossally stupid to marry a man (if married they really were) on four days' acquaintance. Her first major decision made on impulse, and she had screwed it up. Well, perhaps it wasn't surprising; it wasn't like she had much experience with relationships. For all her twenty-eight years she'd only had one or two serious boyfriends, and none of them had lasted very long.

Guy, though—Guy was different. At least she'd thought he was different, yesterday. And that this world was different from where she'd come from. Not just in its landscape and flora and fauna, like that strange bush on the other side of the clearing with its spiky leaves and vaguely-sinister-looking, blood-red berries. She had no idea what it was called, and she was pretty sure it didn't exist in her old world, for all that the climate seemed so similar.

The marriage customs they had here, too—similar, but not similar. She was quite sure that marriage vows *meant* something here. When Guy thought he had unwittingly "trapped" Cat in a marriage to him, he'd been devastated. They didn't start and end relationships here as casually as they did at home... Home? Wait, no, *this* was Cat's home now. Oh dear...

A branch cracked not far off. Cat sat bolt upright and listened. Steps—quietly, stealthily moving through the underbrush...

"Sshhh! Bubba be shush!" came the penetrating stage whisper of a two-year-old. "Mumma wanna be awone!"

Oh. Cat rolled her eyes. It looked like there were some drawbacks to having a tiny stepdaughter with unusual psychic abilities: hiding from her (and, by implication, her father) was proving nearly impossible.

Guy's head came into view, cautiously peering around the trees that marked the entrance to the arbour.

"Sshhh!" hissed Bibby again from her perch on his arm, squishing her chubby little forefinger to her lips.

Cat resignedly shook her head.

"It's okay," she said. "You're here, you might as well come the rest of the way."

Guy put the little girl on the ground.

"Mumma!" she squealed happily and launched herself at Cat. "Mumma no be awone?"

Can picked her up and hugged her. You couldn't be angry with her, she was just so sweet. Bibby's red curls tickled Cat's nose, and she puffed air out of her nostrils. The baby giggled.

"Dat tickles!" she said.

Cat blew a raspberry on the little girl's round cheek. Anything to avoid looking at Guy. What was he doing here, anyway?

He cleared his throat.

"Cat—Catriona?"

Cat looked up at him. His turquoise eyes were on her, uncertain.

"Well?"

"I'm sorry," he said. "I'm sorry I was, uh, abrupt. It's just..."

"Bubba sowwy," explained Bibby, patting Cat's cheek with her little hand.

Cat had to laugh.

"Yes, sweetie, he said so. Why don't you go and find some pine cones to play with? Look, there's a nice one." She put the baby down, then looked back up at Guy. "It's just what?"

He heaved a big sigh.

"It's—well, Ashya. She always wanted more, always. Whatever I had, whatever I did, it was never enough. And then she left. So I was afraid that..."

"That it was starting all over again?" That actually made sense. Cat levered herself up from the rock and stepped in front of Guy, tilting her head back so she could look in his eyes. "Look, Guy," she began. He took a step back. "No," Cat said, stepping closer to him. "Listen to me. You need to get it through your head right now,"—she poked her finger at his chest for emphasis—"that *I am not Ashya*. I'm not your ex-wife. In case you hadn't noticed, I didn't leave. I could have; you gave me that option, remember? You gave me the travel bowl so I could leave. But I didn't. I chose to give it to Sepp instead. Because I'm staying. Do you get it? I'm *staying!*" She gave another jab at his breastbone with her finger.

Guy opened his mouth, but Cat shook her head. "I'm not done yet. Look, it's *because* I'm staying I want that hot water tank. I come from a place where we have everyday stuff you probably can't even imagine here. We have electricity, which means we can have brilliant light, or heat for cooking, by flicking a switch or clicking a button. We have central heating—one touch on a dial, and the furnace starts blowing warm air into the room."

"But..."

Cat pointed her finger. "Still not done. We have bathrooms in every house, often several of them, where we just have to turn a tap and hot water comes gushing out."

Guy blinked. "But..."

"Yes," said Cat, "I know you don't, and you can't, have all of that here—that's not my point. My point is that I don't mind giving up that stuff if I have to, but I do mind if I don't have to. I'm staying here, and staying here with *you*, but I don't want to be uncomfortable for the rest of my life!"

Guy looked down at her with an intense light in his eyes, drawing in a deep breath and blowing it back out. He reached out and cradled Cat's cheek. A tingle ran down her back.

"Catriona..."

Steps sounded through the woods.

"Guy? Catriona? Are you there? Bibby!"

Guy quickly pulled back his hand as Cat turned her head.

"Here, Aunt!" he called, his voice just a little shaky.

Ouska strode into view, her stocky figure encased in her usual outfit of long, tiered skirt and loose blouse, her greying brown hair wound in a coronet of braids around her head.

"Ah, there you are," she said in a satisfied tone. "I thought as much."

Well, yes, she would. She had the same unusual gift as her little great-niece, and as Cat was beginning to discover she had herself. Apparently it came from being an only daughter of an only daughter—an Unissima—and it meant she knew things without being told, particularly things about people she was close to. The Knowing, they called it. Cat had never had that ability back in her old world, but there seemed to be something about this place that brought out those latent gifts in people.

"Hello, Aunt." She smiled at the older woman, and Bibby ran over to clutch at Ouska's skirt.

"Wook!" she said, holding up a pine cone.

"Lovely, dear," said Ouska, her work-worn brown hand stroking the little girl's curly head. "Listen," she turned to her nephew, "Yldra's Randor has been getting into mischief all morning because he's bored; he needs someone to play with. I'll take the little one with me right now. Come, Bibby, we'll go play with Randy, and you'll sleep at Aunt's house tonight."

"Pay Wandy!" agreed Bibby, and she clutched the older woman's hand.

"Uh, yes," said Guy to their retreating backs, "you know where her night shift is? In the chest in the cottage?"

"We'll manage," Ouska said over her shoulder, and she gave them a fleeting smile that almost amounted to a grin.

A slightly awkward silence fell between Cat and Guy as the sound of Bibby's and Ouska's departing steps faded away. They were alone together. For the first time since they had spoken the words of marriage to each other. Just the two of them.

Cat crouched down on the soft forest floor, picking up the pine cone Bibby had left behind. It was a bright reddish colour, the tips shading into black-brown.

"Catriona—" Guy began, his voice a little hoarse. He was looking at the ground in front of him. "Catriona, do you mean it?"

Cat touched the sharp little point on the end of one of the pine cone segments. "Do I mean what I said about staying? Of course I do, or I wouldn't have said it. I..."

"Cat—Cat, you know—you could have anything you want, if I can give it to you, anything to make you comfortable. I..."

"Oh!" Cat looked up at him. "Really? So we can get the water heater?"

"Yes," he said quietly.

"With an indoor bathroom?"

"I suppose, if you want..."

"That's great!" Cat gave him a big smile. Then her eyes began to sparkle. "Anything, you said?"

He nodded. "If I can give..."

Cat talked right over him. "How about we make the cottage bigger? Lots bigger? You know, build another floor on top, or double the floor space? We could knock the whole place down and rebuild!"

"Uh..."

"And put in a dining room with a crystal chandelier!"

"A crystal chande—"

"And oh," continued Cat, "I always wanted a purple silk dress with a really long train! And a tiara to match, gold by preference, with amethysts and princess-cut diamonds and..."

Suddenly she found herself flat on her back, her wrists pinned to the forest floor. Guy's turquoise eyes were shooting sparks mere inches above her own.

"You little tease!" he growled. "You need to be taught a lesson!" He kissed her long and hard on the mouth.

"Oh," Cat squeaked when she could catch her breath, "oh, teacher, sir, I don't think I understood that lesson! Can you please repeat it, sir?"

Sir obliged.

ele

It was a peculiar dream, just sounds—like the old-fashioned radio plays Cat used to listen to when she was a kid.

"Nicky?"

"Oh, it's you! You got back then, did you?"

"Yes, I did. Can I come in?"

"I'm in the middle of something—actually, I'm just leaving, I have to go out of town for a few days. And you just disappeared on me, back there at Ryan's place the other day."

"I'm really sorry about that."

"And what's with that bowl?"

"The bowl? Oh, it's—I'll tell you later. But Nicky, I found Cat! She's back at my home, back in..."

"Oh, whatever. You mean that 'other world' you keep talking about? Sepp, I'm not buying that. My best friend has vanished, and you come along with this rigmarole..."

"Nicky! Nicky, don't cry. Honestly, it's true! I went back to Ruph, and Cat's there, and she's staying—she's with my brother, and..."

"Oh, what, now you're telling me Cat's hooking up with some guy in your mysterious world? Give me a break, Sepp. Cat's not like that. She's got a head on her shoulders. She thinks. She's... Oh, what the heck. Come in then."

The sound of a door clicking shut.

Cat's eyes popped open.

She stared into the darkness around her. Sepp and Nicky. So he made it back to America, had he? And Nicky wasn't having any of his sweet-talking. Cat wasn't surprised. But Nicky had let Sepp into her apartment. Whether she'd ultimately believe him about Cat and Guy and Ruph, that was another matter...

Cat wondered when this conversation had taken place. She had no doubt that it was real, that she had heard something that actually happened. Or, perhaps, it hadn't happened yet? Maybe she was hearing things from the future?

She could just make out the faint outline of the window beside the bed. It was the small hours; dawn had not even begun.

Guy gave a deep snore, then woke up just enough to roll over and fling his arm over her.

"Guy?" Cat said softly.

"Mmm?"

"Are you awake?"

"Mmm." He pulled her closer against him.

"Why did you go to sleep in the workshop last night?"

He made a snuffling noise, then cleared his throat.

"Umm, I didn't... didn't want to bother you." His voice was slow and rough with sleep.

"Bother me?" Cat pushed back and propped herself up on one elbow. "What do you mean, bother me?"

"Well," he mumbled, "sometimes people, uh, sleep better on their own. You know, not, uh..."

That Ashya had a few things to answer for.

"Ah, I see." Cat lay back down. "And did you?"

"Did I what?"

"Sleep better on your own."

He sounded a bit sheepish. "No."

"Me neither." She snuggled up against his warm chest and yawned. "Guy?"

"Hmm?"

"Can you tell how awfully bothered I am right now?"

She could feel the rumble of his chuckle right through his chest.

14

CHAPTER 2

I T WAS THE NEXT day they first saw the grey mice.

Guy had quite the kitchen garden beside the cottage—tangled, overgrown, full of fascinating foodstuffs. Cat gingerly made her way in through the creaking gate, cobbled together from crooked wooden slats. She didn't know a whole lot about gardening, having lived in town all her life, but when she was thirteen or fourteen her grandmother grew tomatoes in pots on the back patio for a couple of years. Cat had loved those fresh-from-the-vine tomatoes. And she had always enjoyed visiting the garden centre by the hardware store, with its humid air so thick with the oxygen the plants breathed out and the trickle of the small artificial fountains they had installed in the corners. But she'd never had a real garden or even been around one much. Here, in Ruph, she thought, the gardens were probably the equivalent of what the grocery store was back where she came from.

Cat carefully picked her way along a path running down the middle of the vegetable patch. The climate here seemed to be quite a lot like the Pacific Northwest, where she came from. It was September, and there were fall vegetables in evidence everywhere, once you spotted them in the tangle of leaves. Squashes grew in the most amazing locations. One vine seemed to have climbed through and around the runner beans that grew in a mound over a bean teepee; there was a pale blue squash hanging about six feet off the ground, surrounded by a mass of bean leaves. *Hah*, thought Cat, *even the squashes are turquoise in a Septimus garden!* This one was a minty blue-green, a funny colour she had never seen on any squash in the supermarket. But then, the beans that were peeking out from under the leaves were purple. Purple beans? Blue squashes? *All that is missing*, Cat thought, *are yellow tomatoes—and what do you know, here they are.* There were some regular round ones—which was how she knew that in spite of their colour they were indeed tomatoes—and next to them were really little ones that were not only yellow, but funny-shaped, like tiny bright golden pears.

Cat reached out her hand for one and brushed against a silvery-green plant next to it. It released a scent that instantly assailed her with the memory of Thanksgiving dinner. Turkey? Why was she thinking of turkey? She took a closer look at the plant, gently petted its thick, velvety leaves, and inhaled the fragrance. Sage! That's what it was; this was a sage plant. *Sage and onion stuffing, mmm.* There was another similar-looking plant, this one with a pattern of purple, silver, and green on the leaves—was it another kind of sage? She reached through the silvery sage for the other plant, when a small, furry shape scurried out from beneath it and ran over her foot.

"Eeek!" She stumbled back, landing in the shrub on the other side of the path. A cloud of sharp peppermint scent rose around her.

"Cat?" Guy come running around the corner from behind the cottage where the privy was, hopped a few steps like he was in a sack race in order to pull up his breeches, and tied up the drawstrings without looking. "Cat! Are you all right?"

Cat started to giggle.

"Yes, yes, I'm fine! I just got scared by a mouse. I don't know where it got to—oh, there it goes! No, there's another one! Three!"

Guy frowned.

"That's odd. I don't remember there being a mouse nest in the garden. Hmph." He took a long-legged stride across the herb bed to reach the path, rubbed his hands on the seat of his breeches and held them out to Cat. "Come on, Madam Wife, don't sit in the peppermint all day. We have places to go and things to do." He pulled her to her feet.

"We do?" she said, beating at the backside of her skirt to get the garden dirt off. It was her own, lovely skirt she had brought from America, not one of his first wife's hand-me-downs. She supposed she had to make do with those for the time being, though; her one outfit wasn't going to go very far, and her skirt was a little shorter than the ankle length women seemed to wear around this place. "So where are we going?"

"Well, we do have a child somewhere we might collect, if she's willing to come home with us. And I was going to see if Aunt has some more bread for us, or perhaps Yldra does. I never did get to making our own yet."

"Hm, yes," Cat said, "I suppose I'll have to figure out how to do that. Where I come from—Eek, another one!"

A little grey mouse scuttled across the path in front of them and vanished into the undergrowth.

Guy laughed.

"You're squeaking. I thought you were a Cat, not a Mouse."

Cat wrinkled her nose at him. "It's a good thing I'm not as skittish about mice as Nicky. She would have shrieked down half the forest by now."

"So... this Nicky, she's your friend?"

They started down the path heading for the village of Ruph. Cat had been there a few times before, to see his aunt and uncle, but their house was at the very outskirts of the village, and she hadn't seen more of the town than that so far.

"Yes, she's my best friend. We met in college. She's..."

"College?"

"It's like school—do you have school here? Except for young adults, not children. You learn skills for work, or you just study. I got an English degree, and Nicky was doing Fine Arts. She works in an interior decorator's office; I think that's where she ran into Ashley—Ashya—before. She wasn't terribly impressed. In fact, not to put too fine a point on it, she said Ashley was the client from hell."

Guy snorted.

"I didn't understand half of what you just said there, but if this 'decorator' thing has anything to do with ornaments, and especially expensive ones, then that's very likely true. Ashya was—is—particular."

"Particular isn't even the word, from what Nicky told me."

He was silent for a moment, carefully stepping across a thick root in his path. He was walking in the underbrush so Cat had enough room on the clear path. *How considerate of him*, Cat thought. *Well, I suppose he could walk in front or behind me, too, but then we couldn't hold hands while we're walking.*

"So what is Nicky like?" Guy asked. "What kind of person is she?"

"Why do you want to know?"

"Sepp," said Guy.

"You mean because he went back to my world because of her? And you're wondering if my friend has nefarious intentions towards your brother?"

"Something like that," he said with a crooked smile.

"To be honest, I can't tell you. Oh, no, I didn't mean it like that! Not nefarious intentions, she wouldn't have. She's not like that. Sure, she's had lots of boyfriends, but..."

"But...?"

"Never someone she could stick with. I guess she just never found the right man yet."

"Demanding, is she?"

"No, not at all. Although she'd have a right to be. She's quite special—she's honest, she's kind, she's fun—and pretty, too, much prettier than me..."

Guy couldn't leave that unchallenged. They didn't even notice the little grey mouse that peered at them from under the leaves beside the path and then quickly scurried back undercover.

When they resumed their walk, their arms firmly around each other's waist, Cat started again. "What was I saying? Oh yeah, Nicky. She's great, really! I think you'd like her. And I think Sepp could be good for her, from what little I've seen of him. He's got a good head on his shoulders, doesn't he?"

Guy snorted. "I suppose he does. And no shortage of self-confidence, usually."

"That's what I mean. Nicky's had a tendency to attract guys that are—not to say losers, but you know what I mean. They trail her like puppy dogs because she's kind and makes them feel special, and she's such an interesting person. But then sooner or later it usually turns out the guy is useless and just needs her as a prop for his own ego. It's like she can't get a man who can stand on his own two feet and look after *her* for a change. Not that she needs looking after, but it would do her good if for once she had a shoulder to lean on." To clarify her point, Cat demonstrated just how to lean on someone's shoulder, which led to another interruption in their progress.

"Hmm," said Guy, when they took to the path again, "you could have a point there about Nicky and Sepp. He's a bit like that too. Not that he's had 'girl friends', as you put it, but there's been more than one girl in the village who's tried to get his attention."

"Kashinka, for one?"

He gave a slight shudder. "Oh yes, dear Kashinka. But others, too. Except so far he's fobbed them off. He never found one he liked enough to step out with more than once or twice—although he's always pleasant enough to them."

"I wonder if the attention he's been getting would have changed, now that it's come out he isn't the Septimissimus after all. I mean, I'm sure Kashinka, for one, was mostly interested in him because she thought he was important. But, poor her, she can't have the real Septimissimus. He's taken."

Guy grinned. "Do I hear a hint of smugness, Madam Wife?"

"Why yes, Sir Husband," said Cat with an answering grin. "I set out to marry this town's most important magical figure—specifically came from Greenward Falls by way of a magical bowl to do so—and had him at my feet within minutes of my arrival. Unconscious and bleeding, but at my feet! And had him proposing marriage not twelve hours later. Do I not have a right to be smug?"

Guy demonstrated his agreement.

CHAPTER 3

M ONICA BAUER SLAMMED HER apartment door
shut. Oh, that Ryan was so annoying! How could
Cat have ever gone out with the guy? And Ashley, good
grief. Good *grief*! Nicky met a lot of self-absorbed people in the course of her career, but that woman took the
cake. She was well-matched with Ryan, that was for sure.
But something weird had gone on between her and Sepp;
Nicky was sure of it. Why else would he have suddenly
skedaddled the way he did? He hadn't even bothered to say
goodbye. Poof, gone. And all Ashley had said, in her vague
voice (she was either bitchy or vague; there didn't seem to
be any middle ground with her), was that he "left".

"What do you mean, he left?" Nicky had asked, and
all she got in return was, "Oh, one minute he was there,
and then he wasn't. But they're like that," and when she
asked *who* was like that, she'd got another vacant stare, and
then Ashley turned her back on her and started whining at
Ryan about a broken fingernail or some such thing.

There was something extremely odd going on here. Had
Ashley met Sepp before? But that didn't seem likely. She

was a model, and a well-known one at that—not quite a supermodel, seeing as Greenward Falls was too small a town to support any such ambitions, but she was heading that way. Stylish, up-to-date, modern as they come. And Sepp, he was rather a mystery. He came from some weird place that Nicky couldn't quite figure out. Her best guess was that it was something like a Hutterite community where they lived really primitively—he had no idea how to work appliances or ride a bus, let alone drive a car. And as for computers or TV, Nicky had finally resorted to the "off" switch to get his attention—Sepp had been glued to the tube for three hours solid, watching whatever junk happened to come on. Perhaps his hometown was some kind of back-to-the-land hippie commune, a leftover from the seventies, cut off from the outside world. The outfit he had worn when she met him had her thinking at first he was a fellow medieval reenactor, but apparently the weekend Renaissance fair had been the first of the kind he had ever seen. He had just "stumbled on it", he had said.

Nicky picked up Sepp's smock-like shirt and his beige drawstring pants from the bathroom floor and dumped them in the laundry basket. He was wearing Jace's jeans and Nike shirt when he left—or perhaps they had been Eddie's; Nicky couldn't remember. Guys were always leaving stuff behind at her place; now she could add Sepp's things to the collection. One of the reenactors would probably go gaga over those clothes; they looked to be handmade from some authentic-looking material, maybe even linen. Definitely no polyester here. Better not put them in the dryer, maybe not even the washing machine.

She suppressed a twinge of regret. Somehow she'd thought Sepp was different from all those other guys. Well, he *was* different—in more ways than one, not just his unusual clothes and lack of understanding of modern technology. There was the fact that he had made no attempt whatsoever to hit on her, never mind to try to get into her bed; Nicky wasn't even sure he was interested in her at all. Except for those looks he gave her... Nicky felt a little shiver run down her spine just at the memory of it. And he was courteous, with a kind of old-fashioned politeness about him, but fun at the same time—there had been a definite glint of mischief in his eyes, and that cute crooked grin... Nicky had felt more comfortable with him than with anyone else before. More than comfortable: she felt safe. She had just started to let herself think that maybe, she could trust him—and then he suddenly booked it. Vanished with no trace.

Well, if that's the kind of person he was, good riddance!

Nicky desperately wished she could talk this over with Cat. Cat would tell her, in that commonsensical way of hers, to not break her heart over someone who wasn't worth it. Not that Nicky was breaking her heart over Sepp, of course. Oh no. But it was the kind of thing Cat would say. Where *was* Cat? What had happened to her? For the hundredth time Nicky replayed last Monday's scenes in her mind: They were supposed to have met at the museum; Cat wasn't there; then Sepp had come out of the museum with Cat's purse and a cock-and-bull story of Cat disappearing into thin air, which was no more believable than the cock-and-bull story of his having been transported to Greenward Falls in some weird magical way from his weird magical homeland. They were probably doing pot or 'shrooms or something in that hippie commune of his if he was used to people swallowing stories like that. Maybe it was a cult? Cat would know; she never got suckered into believing tall stories or urban legends. And she was so good at getting information; she would just go on the Internet and do her research librarian thing and in the space of ten minutes she would be able to tell Nicky if there was a cult of that description and what weird things its members got up to.

Where was Cat? Nicky went into her spare bedroom and stared at the boxes of Cat's stuff piled up along the walls. She bit her lip. Maybe Sepp was right after all? Maybe Cat had gone off somewhere, on an adventure. She so had wanted to after that fiasco with Ryan. They had planned to book her a flight that afternoon, that day she disappeared. But if she had found some reason to suddenly take off without telling Nicky, why would she leave her purse behind? And besides, it just wasn't in character for Cat to do something like that.

Nicky knew that she should call the cops, should have called them right away, as soon as Cat vanished. But Nicky had a problem with the police. To her, they weren't the safe, friendly, helpful people that most kids were taught to trust. She had grown up hiding from cops, not going to them for help. She supposed eventually she would have to, there was no other way, and she told herself that it would be okay. But she'd have to find a cop shop other than the one in town; that one, last she heard, was still the domain of at least two of Charlie's ex-buddies. They'd do anything rather than help a sister of Charles Bauer's, even if it was just a half-sister.

And *what* was that on the top of Cat's box of dishes? Little black specks, round long specks, like black kernels of wheat. It wasn't... it was! Nicky screamed and darted back out of the room. Leaning both hands against the wall in the hallway and dropping her head, she took some deep breaths to calm herself. Mouse poop. There was *mouse poop* in her apartment! Why, why, *why* did those revolting creatures insist on coming after her? Everywhere she went, there were mice. Even if there had never been a mouse in sight in a place, as soon as Nicky moved in, or started working there, or only stayed overnight, a mouse would show up. Mind you, in the last few years, it had become a bit better, and Nicky had thought that this apartment, in which she had lived for nearly a year, was mouse-free. But there it was: evidence that the rodents had once again found Nicky's living space.

She steeled herself. This was Cat's stuff, and she was responsible for it; she could not let it fall to the vermin. And so far, there was only the mouse poop, not the live critters. But where there was poop, there were... She sternly told herself to stop it and forced herself to step back into the room. The box of dishes had a smaller box on top of it, one that seemed to have escaped the rodent ravages yet. Nicky would have to check, though. She picked up the smaller box and heard a jingle. What was in there? She cracked open the flaps of the box. Oh, Cat's instruments! The jingle had come from a small tambourine—Nicky smiled as she remembered the Halloween of their last year in college, when she and Cat had gone as gypsies. Cat had used the tambourine to do a little dance number, and Nicky had played wailing tunes on her flute to go with it. Then she shuddered. The mice had been horrible that year; one had run right under her long gypsy skirts. She could barely stand the thought of it, and forced her attention back to the box to avoid the memory. The tambourine lay on top of a stack of other small percussion instruments, and underneath——underneath was a flute! Nicky hadn't played flute in years now; that Halloween might have been one of the last times she had done so.

She picked up the wooden instrument. It was an interesting piece—really a recorder, not a proper silver flute like the one Nicky used to play, which she had let Charlie pawn one day to pay some people who were, as usual, going to do unspeakable things to him or even kill him if they didn't get the money he owed them for drugs (or whatever else he'd spent it on). He'd promised to high heaven that he would pay her back oh-so-soon; and of course Nicky was still waiting for the cash. No, actually, she wasn't waiting any longer; this was the first time she'd thought of her flute in a long time.

She ran her hand down the length of the simple recorder, and then, on an impulse, put it to her lips. *"Three blind mice, three blind mice..."* There was a rustle and a skittering in between the boxes on the floor. Nicky screeched at the top of her voice, blindly threw the recorder, and ran out of the room, slamming the door behind her.

Cat's stuff would have to take its chances; Nicky was not going to go back in there.

The phone in the living room bleeped.

"Monica Bauer? We have you listed as a next of kin to a Charles Bauer. Is that correct? We are very sorry to tell you there has been an accident..."

CHAPTER 4

NICKY BURIED HER HEAD in her hands. Charlie. Charlie was gone. First Cat disappeared; now this. Charlie hadn't been a good brother—Nicky was under no illusion about this. He'd been a major screw-up, and had made her life difficult in more ways than one. But still, he'd been her brother. Half-brother, anyway. Same dad, different moms. Where Charlie's mom was, who knew; Nicky had a vague memory of hearing that she died of a drug overdose when Charlie was little, before their dad hooked up with Nicky's mother—who, in turn, had taken off to parts unknown when Nicky was in her early years of college; last Nicky had heard, she had been in Mexico somewhere. Or maybe it had been Hawaii? Or the Easter Islands, for all Nicky cared. Dad had more or less drunk himself to death. Charlie had been well on his way to following his example—but it wasn't drinking that had killed him, not directly anyway. A head-on collision, the police said, on the highway. Looked like excessive speed was involved, perhaps even a car chase; witnesses were a bit vague on the issue. And Verena had been in the car with him. Verena—but not Ben. Nicky had only met Charlie's wife once, briefly, after their Vegas wedding; her kid had been ten or twelve. That had been a couple of years ago. Nicky was surprised they had stayed together that long; usually Charlie's girlfriends, or wives—he'd had a couple of the latter, even before Verena—didn't last long. And then, it appeared, he had adopted the kid. Ben Bauer, she supposed he was called now.

And now Nicky was the boy's guardian. She shook her head. It was just too weird. Charlie, adopting a kid? And then making a will, appointing his half-sister as guardian? It seemed very much out of character. But apparently it happened, or the cops wouldn't have called her about it.

So her best friend vanished, then her brother got himself killed, and now she had become guardian to a boy she'd only met once for about five minutes. What was she going to do with the kid? Well, first of all, she'd have to collect him from a town five hundred miles away where he was staying with some neighbours until she came for him. He probably didn't even know who Nicky was, really. Good grief. Poor kid.

She wandered into her bedroom and rummaged in the closet for her overnight bag. She'd have to drive herself; fortunately, it was only September, so the roads over the mountains should be okay. She threw a pair of jeans in the bag, some underwear, a sweater, and an oversized T-shirt by way of a nightie. Her hand brushed up against her black slacks hanging in the closet, and she considered for a moment. Perhaps it would be appropriate to bring something black to wear; there might be a funeral. Or was she supposed to arrange for all that? Maybe the boy would like it. She would not want him to feel that she had no respect for his mom. She folded the slacks and put them in the bag along with a sober-looking beige blouse and a dark blazer she usually wore for business lunches with extra-starchy clients.

Oh, drat—business. She would have to call work and let them know she would be gone for a few days. She ought to be due some bereavement leave; a brother was a first-degree relative, that should be good for about three days, shouldn't it? Even with her boss being as sticky as she was about these things. Nicky sighed. Cat had been right about chucking up her job at the library the way she did. Even at the time, Nicky had wondered if she should follow her friend's example and just quit work so they could go off adventuring together. But it had taken her long enough to nail down that job at GreenFall Interior Design, and she did enjoy the design part of it. She hated dealing with the snooty clientele, though. Unfortunately, interior design businesses attracted snooty rich folk by default; nobody else could afford their services. What Nicky really wanted was to create for theatre productions or movies, or for historic reenactments—she wanted to make surcoats and liripipes and soft flowing dresses, or design wall hangings and heavy carved furniture to go into beautifully shaped large chambers. But work like that was impossible to find, especially in places like Greenward Falls (population fifty thousand). And now, Nicky supposed, she was stuck for good. If she had to look after a kid to boot, how was she supposed to support them? Her paycheque was only just

31

enough to cover her rent and food, with a bit left over for other living expenses. Ah well. Nicky squared her shoulders. She would cross that bridge, and every one after that, when she came to it.

Suddenly, out of nowhere, the memory of Sepp assailed her. What would he make of this, of her criminal brother who had gotten himself killed on the highway and left her a kid to look after? Nicky had a feeling that the criminal element wasn't something Sepp was all that familiar with. There had been a certain amount of innocence, or naivete, under that shrewdness and common sense of his. There was that twinge of regret again. Where *had* the guy gone so suddenly? Ryan was offensive, and Ashley even worse, but was that a reason for Sepp to just up and vanish from their place? Nicky shook her head, then ran all ten fingers through her tangle of blonde curls. She would *forget* Sepp. She had other things to think about.

There was a knock on her apartment door. Now what? Nicky went to the peephole and peered through. She couldn't see a thing. Oh, right. She had hung a dream catcher on the outside of the door, and it was covering up the lens. She pulled the door open.

No way. Talk of the devil—well, think of him, anyway. A white Nike shirt, dark jeans, high-top runners. Black, longish hair, and eyes a weird bright turquoise colour. Clutching a blue-green pottery bowl as if it were some special treasure.

No, she would *not* act pleased. She would keep it together. She would show him she didn't need him...

"Nicky?"

"Oh, it's you! You got back then, did you?"

CHAPTER 5

*T*HE SOUND OF A *car engine running and the car radio playing.*

Nicky's voice: "Do you mind that station, Ben? You can change it if you'd rather listen to something else."

"No, it's okay, Aunt Monica."

"You don't need to call me 'Aunt'. Or 'Monica'. Just call me Nicky. I guess I am your aunt, technically, by adoption anyway, but it makes me feel old if you call me that. I'm not that ancient—just twenty-six. So how old are you exactly?"

"Fourteen. Well, pretty soon."

"Oh yes, I saw your birth certificate. On the twenty-fifth, right?"

"Yeah."

"We'll have to celebrate, you and me. And maybe Sepp if he's still around. I told you about Sepp, right?"

"I think so—he's your boyfriend, right?"

"NO!! Sorry, no. Didn't mean to yell. He's a guy that just showed up a couple of weeks ago, when my friend Cat disappeared, and then he disappeared too, and now he's come back, and says he knows where Cat is. He's really weird,

in one way, but in another way, I kind of trust him. Hey, I don't need to tell you all this, I don't want to bore you."

"It's okay, I don't mind." A loud yawn.

Nicky's laugh. "Sure you don't; I'm obviously thrilling you with my story!"

A chuckle in the slightly hoarse adolescent voice. "I'm just tired. Last night was a bit late. So this Seth guy is still at your house?"

"Sepp. Well, we'll have to see if he's still there when we get home, won't we. He came back just after I got the phone call about—well, the phone call. And I asked him to stay and watch the apartment and let in the cable guy to fix the net. Sheesh, at least I can talk to you about this without having to explain everything like to a caveman! Sepp's weird—I'm not sure where he's from, but wherever it is, they live totally off the grid: no power, no indoor plumbing, no cars, nothing. He's got no clue what the Internet is, and the TV was this huge revelation to him. You should have seen him when I took him on the city bus... Oh. You're asleep. That's just as well. Okay, another couple of hours should get us home."

The sound of the car engine fading out.

"...so we're having the stove and the water heater installed today," Cat said to Ouska. "It's going to be almost the same as yours. And we'll have a little bathroom space in part of the workshop; Guy is moving the pottery wheel over a few feet to make space for it. I can't wait to have a nice bath again, and be able to wash Bibby without having to boil the kettle over the fire for warm water!" She was leaning against the table in Ouska's kitchen, contemplating the closed stove with the enamel tank over it that delivered warm water to the bathroom on the other side of the wall.

"That'll be nice, with the cooler weather setting in," said Ouska. "And baking your own bread will warm the place nicely. I could have shown you how to bake bread in a pot on the hearth, too, but it's more fuss than the stove."

Cat took the striped apron Ouska handed her and tied it around her middle. "I sure appreciate you keeping us supplied with bread the last few weeks; it's been hard enough learning to cook stew in the open fireplace. I mean, not that Guy was asking me to, but I want to. He's still better at it than I am—or at making porridge, for that matter. Good thing he's not a picky eater."

Ouska gave a dry chuckle. "No, he was capable enough at caring for himself and the babe before you came, and that woman certainly didn't spoil him with her cooking." Guy's aunt rarely referred to his first wife by her name, she still resented her for how she had treated her favourite nephew and then just abandoned him and their little daughter. "Very well. Sourdough."

She picked up a stoneware crock from the shelf above the fireplace and brought it over to the heavy deal kitchen table, then took a large brown mixing bowl from the top of the Welsh dresser.

Cat rapped her knuckles on the edge of the bowl and smiled at the deep bell-like ring that came from it. "I think that's the biggest piece of Guy's I've seen yet," she said. "That's got to be, what, twenty inches across at the top?"

"It's a good pot," Ouska said. "Nice and sturdy."

She took the lid off the sourdough crock, and Cat peered in.

"This looks like my porridge from this morning," she said, "it was too runny again. But this stuff bubbles. And it smells like beer."

"That's the sourdough working," said Ouska. "Sometimes I've used some of Uncle's beer leaven if he had extra, it's quicker to make bread with that, it'll rise faster. But this works, and it's simple."

"Leaven? Oh, I think we call it yeast where I'm from. So you don't need to add any of that? I thought you couldn't make bread without it."

"There's enough leaven in the air, if you know how to catch it and feed it." Ouska poured some of the sourdough into the bowl, then took the salt cellar from the cupboard and sprinkled a few spoonfuls over the sloppy sourdough. She pointed Cat to the flour bin that stood in the corner. "We need two scoops of flour," she said.

Cat grabbed the large wooden scoop that was stuck in the top of the wholemeal flour that filled the bin halfway.

"This is a nice bin," she said, dumping a scoop of flour into the bowl. "Is it new?"

"Yes, we just had it built. The vermin chewed a hole into the flour sack I had before; most of the flour was spoiled. So we got something more solid."

"Guy says the mice are way worse this year than ever before. They made a total mess of the last loaf of bread you gave us; it was horrible. Chewed up, peed on, totally disgusting—we had to throw it out. So gross."

"Yes, they're bad this year," said Ouska. "I don't remember them ever as bad as this. And they're a different kind—grey or black, not the normal brown wood mice. Our little cat is a good mouser, but she can't keep up, and Yldra says her three cats are becoming downright fat with all the mice they're getting. One of them even caught a rat the other day. I don't think the mice are quite as bad further out of town, but the boys had a goodly part of their corn storage spoiled."

"The boys?"

"My boys, Charn and Chonyk, on the farm."

"Oh, I don't think I've met them yet—have I? Guy's got so many cousins..."

"No, I suppose you haven't, then. Charn said they had close on five-score mice in their smaller granary, the one that's not built as tight as the new one. Guy's father helped build the bigger one, and you know he had that knack of making things fit and work right. So no vermin get into that one, thank goodness, or there would have not even been any seed corn left for next season."

She rolled up the sleeves of her blouse and plunged her hands into the flour in the bowl. "Now this is where the real work begins," she said, stirring the dough with both hands. "Here, give it a try." She rubbed the sticky dough off her fingers.

Cat stuck her hands into the sticky batter and squished and stirred until all the dry flour had disappeared into it,

Ouska sprinkling additional flour in until the dough was no longer sticky.

"Now, move the bowl over a bit," said Ouska. She scooped a handful of flour from the bin and sprinkled it on the surface of the table, then took the lump of dough from the bowl and smacked it on the table. "Ever done any kneading before?"

"A bit," said Cat. She grasped the dough and started rolling it towards her.

Ouska chuckled. "You're kneading like a potter," she said. "You don't need to make a nice little roll of it like your man does with his clay; with bread, it doesn't matter how you handle it, so long as you do it hard." She tore the lump of dough in half and showed Cat what she meant.

"Oh, I get it!" said Cat. She lifted the dough lump and smacked it on the table so hard the crockery on the dresser rattled.

"Well done," said Ouska. "It will rise nicely if you keep that up."

"The harder you whack it, the better it gets?"

"That's about the size of it," replied the older woman.

"So, Aunt," said Cat, pummelling, squishing, and pounding the dough, "there was something I've been meaning to ask you."

"Yes?" said Ouska, looking up from her kneading.

"You know, being an Unissima—do you sometimes have special dreams?"

"Dreams?" The older woman took Cat's piece of dough, smacked the two lumps back together, kneaded them into a ball, and put it in a bowl on the warming shelf by the stove. "That'll need to rise for a few hours now," she said. "What kind of dreams do you mean?"

"Well, something to do with the Knowing. Twice now I'm sure I heard them in my sleep, Sepp and my friend Nicky. You know he took that last travelling bowl and went back to my world; he had some unfinished business there with Nicky. And I think I've heard them in a dream. Only heard them, though, I don't see anything when I do—that's one of the things that's different from normal dreams. In fact, I think I had another kind of dream earlier that was the opposite, I only saw images, but didn't hear anything, and it wasn't anyone I knew, or a place I had ever seen. But in these, I recognize their voices. And I'm sure it's real."

"Hmm," said Ouska, rubbing her hands clean on her apron. "I can't say I've ever had a dream like that, but that's not to say that it couldn't happen to you. The Knowing can take different forms. There," she said, handing Cat a jug, "we need to feed the sourdough. Get it about half full of warm water, would you?"

Cat collected the water from the tap in the bathroom behind the kitchen, and Ouska mixed the water with some more flour into the remaining sourdough in the crock. "So you are certain you have been hearing the boy and your friend?"

Cat smiled—Guy was nearly thirty, his brother not much more than a year younger, but to their aunt they were still "boys". "Yes, it's definitely them. And I know that what I'm hearing is actually happening—or maybe has happened, or will happen; that part I haven't figured out—but it's real."

Ouska put the sourdough crock on the warming shelf beside the mixing bowl. "Now," she said, "by tomorrow it will have worked through nicely, and we can make another batch of bread if we need to. So that's all there is to bread making, other than rising and baking it. Well, I cannot help you with those dreams, but by the sounds of it, you already know what to make of them."

"Yes," said Cat slowly, "I suppose I do, really. I guess you have to learn a lot of this for yourself, don't you? Not like baking bread."

The older woman smiled. "Well, bread I can teach you; the Knowing, not so much. I can only tell you how mine works, but yours might be quite different. Although once you learn how to deal with something, no matter how, it's all the same—you do it without thinking. Bread's like that, and the Knowing is too."

"Okay," said Cat, "so let me write down the bread recipe. Do you have some writing stuff?"

Ouska gave a chuckle. "Oh yes, you have that madness for writing things down. Let me see, I know I have some paper—and I'm sure there is pen and ink here someplace." She went into the sitting room and came back with a sheet of coarse-looking brown paper, an ink bottle, and a pen. "There, I knew Uncle kept some about."

Cat took the cork out of the ink bottle and dipped the pen in. "So, let me get this straight. About three or four cups of sourdough?"

"Yes, about that. And as much flour to start with, and then however much it takes to make a firm dough. Don't forget to write down the salt; it's a mite bland without it."

Cat copied it out.

"How long does it need to rise?" she asked.

"Oh, a few hours. Until it's about twice as big as it was."

Let rise until doubled in bulk, Cat wrote.

"Then what?"

"Then punch it down, shape it, rise it again, and bake it."

"For how long, and how hot?"

"Well, at middling heat, until it's ready—"

Cat snorted. "You sound like my grandmother. I once asked her how to make turkey stuffing, and she said, 'Oh, it's easy, you just do it!'"

Ouska smiled. "Well, then, say, half an hour or so. You have to keep turning it in the oven; I'll show you."

Cat finished her recipe sheet:

Bake for half an hour at moderate h-

"Drat!" she said, "ink blot! And I was doing so well, too! It's not easy writing with these pens, you know. They splatter. And I think the ink is almost out."

"We'll have to make some more then. Or better yet, ask Nikor Archivist, he might let us have some. I can give him some of Uncle's applejack in trade, and he loves my quince preserve; I might promise him a jar or two when I make it next week. Come to think of it—" Ouska gave Cat a considering look. "With your passion for writing things down, it's high time you met Nikor."

"Archivist? What does he do?"

42

"Keep the archives, of course. You've been to the library, have you not?"

"Not really. Guy pointed it out to me the other day, but we were on our way to meet the second or third dozen relatives who hadn't seen me yet, so we didn't have time for more than that. And besides—" Cat suddenly felt a little shy. "Well, I'm a librarian. I kind of have high expectations on libraries..."

"Don't fret," said Ouska, patting Cat on the shoulder, "Nikor keeps a good library, for all he's getting on in years. In fact, we could go over there right now; the bread will be a few more hours."

"Oh!" Cat said, "I hadn't expected—but, all right, why not?" She blew on the recipe sheet to dry the ink. "There. They say that the faintest ink is better than the strongest memory. Let's go see this library."

CHAPTER 6

"THERE IT IS," SAID Ouska, gesturing at the large half-timbered building on the south side of the marketplace and the square structure set at a right angle to it. "And that's the hall, of course."

"They're quite the impressive buildings," said Cat, climbing up the broad stairs after the older woman.

"Yes, the library and the hall were built around the same time. The Septimus of the time figured they might as well be made large and solid, to last."

Ouska pushed open the heavy carved double doors. They stepped into the hush of library buildings everywhere, and Cat's nose tingled at the scent of paper and bindings. *I've missed this*, she thought. Most of the bookshelves were mounted onto the walls of the large room, its ceiling coffered in well-aged wood. Along the right-hand wall, three or four stacks jutted out into the room at right angles, ending a few feet away from a solid reading table in the middle of the room, directly beneath a skylight through which the filtered light of the morning sky shone into the room. Brass candlesticks stood on the age-darkened polished surface.

"Nikor Archivist?" called Ouska, making Cat jump. Calling out loud, in a library! Sacrilege! On the other hand, there didn't seem to be anyone there; the place was empty, and the sound of Ouska's call was muffled by the heavy leather bindings of the books. Calling out in an empty library wasn't really as sacrilegious as all that.

It's like one of those old university libraries, thought Cat, *or a monastery in the Middle Ages. Except that the books aren't chained to the tables.*

A rustling sound came from the stacks, and Cat caught a glimpse of movement.

"Nikor! Nikor Archivist, I've brought someone to meet you," Ouska called again.

A small apparition shuffled into view. No more than five feet tall, the librarian of Ruph was a wizened little man with a fringe of silver hair setting off the deep mahogany of his bald pate. He peered at them nearsightedly over a stack of books that he was balancing under his chin.

"Oh! Ous-Ouska Wisewoman! I will just, just put these—" He shuffled over to the heavy reading table, and, precariously balancing the books on one hand, felt around the table with the other, pushing one of the brass candlesticks out of the way. The book stack began to slide, and Cat, without thinking, jumped and caught it. The weight of the heavy tomes nearly knocked her over, but the instinct from years of practice with juggling book piles asserted itself. She straightened herself and the volumes, and carefully set them on the library table.

Nikor Archivist blinked at her. "Thank you, thank you," he said. "These are the stories of Dohidil and Ruhiramy, the brothers who found the Stone of Kelosia. They were lost between the books of herb and stone lore, stone lore, and who put them..."

"Nikor Archivist," interrupted Ouska firmly, though not unkindly, "this is Catriona Potterswife. I brought her to see the books, and to meet you."

"Books, books books. Yes. Potterswife? Ah! Young Dyniselm Potter. Potterswife, from Outland, yes?" He blinked at Cat in what seemed a rather pleased fashion.

"Yes," said Cat, "yes, I do come from Outland! Do you know it?"

"King Arthur," said the librarian, "Geoffrey of Monmouth. Troubadours, Walter von der Vogelweide. Yes yes. Marco Polo? Yes, Polo. But that was long ago. We have a manuscript. Have they discovered printing in Outland yet?"

"Printing?" Cat said, a little taken aback. "You mean, as in, the printing press?"

"Yes, yes, the press! We have had it for, oh, centuries here. Have Outlanders?"

Cat bit back a chuckle. "Yes, we have had it for nearly six hundred years! Since the fifteenth century, in fact."

"Good! Good good." The librarian was shuffling the books on the table and now peered closely at the second to last one from the bottom. Suddenly he let out a sharp hiss.

"Look!" he cried indignantly, "look!" as he pointed at the corner of the book. Cat bent closer. The edge of the paper had a gouge in it, an uneven hole, like a bite mark.

"Mice!" muttered Nikor disgustedly, "mice mice! In the library!"

Cat gasped. "No! Why, the damage they could do! That's horrible!"

The librarian peered up at her. "You know books, Potterswife?"

"Catriona," interjected Ouska, "her name is Catriona. Yes, she knows books; she is a librarian herself. She has a passion for writing things down, so I brought her here to meet you. I also need ink, Nikor—what would you have in return?"

"Ink?" the librarian echoed distractedly. "Mice!" he muttered again under his breath. "Mice? Ink! You have a cat, Ouska Wisewoman? Library needs a cat. Old Mouser went last spring. Need a new cat."

Ouska raised her eyebrows. "I could find you a cat, Nikor, I think. My daughter's cat just had kittens. I'm sure she would be glad to let you have one."

"Daughter. Young Yldra? Yes. Please to speak to her. Mice!" He shook his head in disgust.

"I need to run an errand or two," said Ouska to Cat. "Do you want to stay here while I do?"

"Yes, I think I do!" said Cat. "It's really good to be around books again…"

"Very well then. Nikor Archivist, do show Catriona around the library. I think she can be of help to you."

Nikor had begun to shuffle back towards the stacks and didn't appear to have heard her. Cat scooted after him.

"Where were those books?" she asked when she caught up with him. "Perhaps there was only one mouse and there isn't much more damage. But it's important to check; if you have old archival materials here..."

He looked at her as if he had already forgotten she was there, and blinked a few times. Suddenly something seemed to register.

"Librarian, are you? Know books? Well! Well well! Come, this way."

He led her between the shelves, which were tightly packed with volumes bound in leather and cloth. *No paperbacks here,* Cat thought, *just good, solid hardcovers.* The smallest of the books were the size of a standard hardbound book, many of them more along the lines of a college textbook. They were heavy volumes that looked like something out of a museum—but books, books nonetheless. Cat was ecstatic.

"What are your holdings here? Is it all nonfiction, or fiction as well?"

"Fiction?" The little librarian sounded puzzled.

"Stories—made up tales, narrative? We call it fiction where I come from. And true accounts, facts, are non-fiction. You spoke of herb lore? That would be non-fiction. 635.7, herbs," she added softly.

"What's that? Six-thirty-five?"

"Oh, sorry," said Cat, "that's just the call number we had assigned to it. Every book is given a number, and we sort them on the shelf by that number. 635.7 is the number for books on herbs. Stone lore, or what we would call mineralogy, is 549."

"Ah!" said Nikor, apparently quick at understanding when the matter at hand was to do with books. "Sort them by a number, eh? So will not lose tales of heroes, heroes, amongst herb and stone lore."

"No, not if we keep the library properly in order. We put the numbers on the spine, which makes it easier; I don't think you could do that with these volumes. The leather or cloth of the covers wouldn't hold the labels."

"No," he said, "no no. But will likely find a way to add the numbers. No?" He peered up at Cat, who felt positively gargantuan standing at five feet six next to this tiny man.

"We probably could," she replied. "Sure, why not? Perhaps write the numbers on the inside. It would be a lot of work though, going through the whole library. Isn't it sorted at all yet?"

"Oh, yes yes, of course, sorted. Herb and stone lore, see." He pointed to a spot on the shelf. A gap in the row of books showed where he had found the mouse-nibbled book that had so incensed him. Cat looked into the gap, sniffed, and recoiled. The rank smell of mouse urine was overpowering, and the shelf was littered with the small black kernels of mouse poop and chewed-up bits of paper and leather bindings.

"Oh dear, this is awful," she said. "We'll have to go through all those shelves and check them; the mice have been having a feast in here. I hope they didn't get at anything really valuable. For starters, we need to set a mouse trap—and definitely get that cat." *Did I just say 'we'?* she thought.

"Yes, cat. Cats. Birds, dogs, dragons," Nikor explained, pointing at various shelf sections where books on these topics were kept.

"Dragons? They would come under mythology and folklore in my old world!" said Cat. "Are they real here?"

"Oh, yes, yes. Perhaps. I think," he said dismissively, shuffling around to the next set of shelves.

Cat smiled. He reminded her of one of her college professors—completely uninterested in whether information was factual, so long as he had a good way of classifying and shelving it.

"Here," Nikor said proudly, waving his hand at two rows of books handsomely bound in leather with what looked like gold tooling on the back, "Chronicles of Ruph. Still writing it. Do you write? Yes, Ouska Wisewoman said so. Will be very good, another set of hands to write."

Cat twisted her mouth a little ruefully. It seemed she had got herself a new job.

Nikor took the last book in the row off the shelf; its cover was deep red and looked quite new. He opened it to show unlined pages, closely written on in a spidery hand, and he turned to the last filled page.

"Must enter marriage soon, haven't written records yet." He handed her the book.

"So you keep records, as well as keeping the books in order?"

"Yes, yes. Chronicler, archivist. Keep books, sort books. Teach younglings to read, to write. Young Dyniselm Potter," he said suddenly, "he read yet? Could never make sense of words, said they jumped. Jumped! Likely enough lad, though."

"Well, he says he still has trouble with them. We call it dyslexia in my old world; some people are just born with it."

"True, true. A bright lad, is Dyniselm Potter. Clay and craft lore, here." He pointed at another section of the shelf. "Ink!" He suddenly remembered. "Ouska Wisewoman wants ink. Shall have to make some. What is the season? Ink time, soon, the nuts are falling."

"Nuts?" asked Cat, "what do nuts have to do with it?"

"Use them to make ink, don't we," Nikor said. "Nut husks, boil them, put in rust. Good ink, that. Time for it soon."

CHAPTER 7

"*D*EAR SON, I SEND *this message with a caravan of traders which is shortly to make its way to the mountains. I hear they carry quantities of fragrance wood at reasonable cost; be sure to secure a portion of it. You have always liked your apples stewed with fragrance wood, and I recently heard tell of a delectable method of making a pumpkin sweet with it as well. Perhaps your wife might prepare it for you. Your Uncle tells of your happiness with Catriona. I am pleased to hear that small Ysbina has found a good mother in her. I wish I could come to Ruph to meet my new son's-wife daughter, but you know Yeryl needs me. The five youngsters are taking much of her strength, and her time is coming nearer, we are expecting the new little one by the winter solstice. But I must come to the point of this missive: your brother-in-law bids me tell you that on your Uncle's return to Ruph he will be sending with him a youngling he has indentured to him but who is of no use in the ironmongery or the counting house, as he will not speak and has little aptitude for figures. The terms of the agreement require the lad to be apprenticed to one of our* *family, and Kaltbur claims you owe him a favour from long ago. He will be sending the lad's apprenticeship fee with him and considers this to absolve him of any further terms of the agreement. I must conclude, as the trader's boy is waiting. Be secure in the favour of the elements, affectionately, your Mother."*

Cat looked up from the letter she had been reading out loud to Guy and folded it back up into a neat little square.

"When was your mother here last?" she asked.

"She moved to Ilim shortly after Father died, to help Yirry with the kids. She likes it there—she came from Ilim herself when she was young, so she still has lots of friends there. And I think she has more fun with her grandchildren than she ever did with us when we were small. Well, there were so many of us, and then there's the burden of being Septimuswife."

"Is that a burden?" wondered Cat. "I haven't found it so——does that mean I'm slacking off? Is there something I'm supposed to be doing to help?"

Guy grinned his crooked grin. "Not that I know of," he said, "but Mother is liable to find things burdensome. She makes work for herself where it isn't called for. But then, I'm still not sure of own task as Septimissimus. Oh, did I say? I am trying the Septimus glaze again. With the firing I did yesterday the kiln should be ready to be opened soon; we'll see if it turned out."

"The Septimus glaze? The turquoise one on the travelling bowls, made from the ash of the Septimus Tree branch? Oh, Guy! That's a bit scary... but really exciting, too! I wonder if it'll do something special again?"

"We won't know until we open the kiln, will we," he said soberly. The special powers he held as seventh son of the seventh son were still so new to him, he was unsure of what exactly they entailed. "I just felt it was time to try again. Things seem to be settling out, even in the workshop. I haven't had any of those holes in my pots since the day we were married. Perhaps it comes from having a bookwoman in the house who reads to me." He gave her a lopsided smile. "My gift no longer reads the words wrong."

Cat smiled back. His misdirection of his gift, a gift he had been unaware he possessed, had resulted in some strange phenomena in his pottery. Some of his work had had holes, which Cat was sure was a misfiring from his being meant to make things *whole*. She was glad to hear that the issue was resolving itself, although she was sure it was not on account of her presence in the house, but because he was no longer suppressing the power that was trying to assert itself in him.

"So what's this favour you owe your brother-in-law?"

"Oh, that!" Guy grinned broadly. "I expect he still hasn't forgiven Sepp and me for hiding in the bushes and making noises like a lovesick tomcat when he was courting Yirry. It threw her right out of her romantic frame of mind; he had a to-do getting her to pay attention to the sweet nothings he wanted to whisper in her ear, never mind listen to his proposal. But seeing as she's been married to him for going on fifteen years, you'd think..."

"What a pair of brats you were!"

"Oh, quite. At twelve and thirteen, you can be pretty inventive. If we'd tried that on any of our brothers, they

54

would have tanned our hides, so we found an easier target."

"Boys..." Cat shook her head. "So, speaking of which, it sounds like you're getting an apprentice! What's the deal with that? Do you have to take him on, favour or not, or could you pawn him off on one of your brothers, say, Chelm, or Yokan?"

"Not Chelm. If the lad was no good in Kaltbur's ironmongery shop, that would say he has no affinity to metal. He would be of no use in the smithy."

"Hmm, I got the impression that your brother-in-law only found him of no use in the shop because he wouldn't talk—I can see that being a problem in a store, where you're supposed to be serving customers."

Guy nodded.

"I wonder what your mother means, 'he doesn't talk'. Or rather, 'will not speak'. Why not, I wonder? Can he not, or will he not?"

He shrugged. "We'll have to see, won't we."

Cat drained the last of the mintbrew from the bottom of her mug. "But what do you mean about 'no affinity to metal'?"

"Well, we are all born with our gifts, aren't we? Those who deal in metal have a bent towards metal. So a boy who is ill at ease in an ironmongery shop won't be a likely apprentice for a blacksmith. We'll have to see if he is of use in the pottery. I must say, an extra pair of hands for the heavy work would not come amiss, particularly now that I have other work to do besides—whatever that may turn out to be. We'll have to find a place for the lad to sleep."

"Oh, you have to house and feed an apprentice, too?"

"Yes, that's why there is a fee for apprenticing. I wonder how long the lad has been with Kaltbur and how much of the fee has been used up. If he's anything like I was as a youngling, he'll be eating through the rest of it fast enough. I'm glad to hear there is some of the money left, at any rate."

Cat got up off the bench and bent over Guy from behind to give him an upside-down kiss. "Can I come watch you unload the kiln? I want to see how those Septimus pots turned out."

CHAPTER 8

"So the Septimus pots are cups this time, not bowls," Cat explained to Ouska as they were walking along to the market square. "The glaze turned out that same amazing turquoise as the travelling bowls were before they got used up and lost their powers. I'm glad, because that is one beautiful glaze—the same colour as their eyes, Guy's and Bibby's and Sepp's. I was sorry it turned that rusty brown when the powers went out of the bowls."

"It's curious the powers went with the glaze," Ouska said, hitching her market basket higher on her arm. "Never saw anything like it before."

"No? I was wondering. We still haven't figured out if there is anything special about the cups, but I think there is. I'm quite sure it's not the same as the bowls, you know, that they take you to a different place if you really want to go, but there's *something*—I can feel it when I hold them."

"Yes," said Ouska, "that's just how it was for those bowls. I only had to hold them to know what worked."

"I know," said Cat, "that's why I brought one of the cups along; I left it back in your kitchen. I want you to take a look at it, maybe you can figure out how it works. I have an inkling, but this Unissima thing is still so new, I don't really know what I'm doing yet. Bibby might understand the cups, too, but she probably couldn't say so, and at any rate, I'm not going to let my toddler play with experimental magic."

Ouska gave an amused snort. "You have odd ways of putting things at times, Catriona—odd, but apt. But yes, it's likely best not to let the babe at those cups until we know what they do. We don't want her vanishing into another world of a sudden."

"No—no, she wouldn't, but who knows what the cups would do. Make her fly, or something."

They were still chuckling when they rounded the corner into the market square. The vendors of Ruph had opened up their sales booths along the sides of the town square as they did every week; some of the stalls, now that the weather was turning colder, were enclosed on three sides in wooden walls, with a solid roof over top. Several of them even had braziers burning in them to give the sellers some extra warmth. That morning there had been a sharp frost, and even now there was still a nip in the air.

"I need to get these dishes to Yokan," Cat said to Ouska, gesturing at her basket. "He promised us some dried fish and said he'd put a fresh carpling aside from the fish pond. I think we'll have it fried for supper. And in turn he's been waiting for that set of pots to make pickled fish in. I think they use it for the solstice feast, don't they?"

"Ah yes, pickled carp, it's a right treat, that, with a chunk of bread."

"How is it made? Like regular pickles?"

"You just take the fish and put it in brine of vinegar, salt, and spices. Oh, and onions. Lots of onions."

"Hmm, sounds interesting. I think we call it rollmops where I come from. Okay, I'm off to shop; meet you in a bit."

The women went their separate ways on their errands. Cat stopped at her brother-in-law's to make her trade, pots for fish, then at the baker-cum-miller's stall for some flour and a few cakes with dried apricots for Bibby and Guy; it was one of their favourite treats. She shook her head at the cost—the price of flour had doubled in the last few weeks, as the mice had been getting into the grain stores all over town. A sizeable lump of cheese from the dairyman's was added to the waxed-paper-wrapped fish in the bottom of her basket; a cabbage and some pears from one of the farmers landed on top. Cat wanted to try cooking the pears with a bit of cinnamon—*fragrance wood*, she mentally corrected herself; that's what her mother-in-law had called it. Guy would enjoy that; he had quite the sweet tooth. The haberdasher's netted her some mending thread and a ball of knitting wool—the toque she was making for her husband was nearly finished, and she was planning on a set of mittens to go with it.

It was when she was haggling with the stationer about the price of a notebook covered in thin brown leather that Cat finally realized what had been bothering her. Someone was staring at her—in fact, had been following her around the market. She had seen him out of the corner of her eye a few times, but now she turned and looked fully at the man, who was loitering around the ironmongery stall next to the stationer's. He was handsome, in a manner of speaking, but there was something about his features —his nose was on the large side, his ears stuck out just a bit, and his black hair sprung back from a forehead that was sloping back just a little. It reminded Cat of something not entirely pleasant, but she couldn't put her finger on just what.

The man saw Cat's eyes on him; pulled back his lips in a semblance of a grin, exposing prominent front teeth; and seemed just on the point of speaking when a progressively louder noise from the street leading up to the marketplace caught everyone's attention.

"Halloo!" hollered a familiar voice amidst the clopping of horses' hooves and the jingling of harness bells, "hullo halloo, Ruph!"

"It's Uncle! I didn't know he was coming back today!" Cat said happily as she snatched up her basket and went to greet Guy's favourite relative. Ouska got there before her and watched as her husband swung himself down from the seat of a heavy horse-drawn carriage.

"So you've come back, have you?" she said, the pleased smile on her face giving the lie to her indifferent tone of voice.

"Yes, woman, I've come back!" he called out. "And a damn long road it was too! I need a rest. I brought your young man's young man along, too," he said to Cat, "and could hardly bear his constant chattering on the way!" He pointed at a dark-haired boy who was perched on the driver's seat, holding the reins of the cart and looking at them from under a pair of black eyebrows.

"What? I thought—oh, you're having me on again! Guy's mother wrote that he doesn't speak."

Uncle laughed heartily, never so pleased as when he managed to pull one over on Cat.

"I'll take the lad back to the house," he boomed to his wife. "When you are done spending all our money, I will see you there."

"Very well, get along with you," said the wisewoman. "Catriona and I will be there shortly."

Uncle caught the harness of the horse and pulled it, clip-clopping, across the marketplace and down the lane that led to his house at the edge of town. Cat looked after them, her eyes lingering on the boy that was to be Guy's apprentice and a part of their family. *If this was my old world, I'd say he's Italian or Greek,* she thought, *or maybe even Indian, with that olive skin and those black eyes and hair.* Something nagged at the back of Cat's mind, as if she had seen the boy somewhere before. *I do hope this works out,* she thought; *he looks a bit unapproachable with that hooked nose of his.*

Cat turned around to get back to the stationer's. The staring stranger had vanished; looking around the market, she couldn't see him anywhere. She wondered briefly about the vague sense of unease that had come with him; it didn't just originate from the man's stare hitting the back of her head. But she didn't think about it long, and got back to her bargaining with Atyrra Paperseller. They finally came to a mutually agreeable deal, and Cat added the notebook to the wool and thread in the leather pouch she was wearing around her waist by way of a purse.

She waited until Ouska was done her shopping, and together they set out for the wisewoman's home.

They heard the singing from several houses away—a loud, insistent song on the pleasures of the vine and the brew, halloo, halloo. Uncle's voice, unmistakably. The women looked at each other with raised eyebrows.

"What is this?" Ouska picked up her pace. As she stepped over the doorsill, she was pounced on and enveloped in a great bear hug, then kissed soundly on the lips. Cat, who was just a few steps behind her, was taken aback. She had never seen Uncle be quite so demonstrative—what was going on here? Ouska gave her husband a cuff on the shoulder, and he reeled, clutching at the kitchen table for support.

"Ooh yes, my woman, my good woman!" he sang out. "How I have missed my good woman!" He dropped heavily into the chair at the end of the table.

"What *have* you been doing?" asked Ouska, sniffing the air, her forehead wrinkled in a formidable frown. "You cannot have got yourself drunk in the short time you have been home! What have you been about?"

Uncle crossed his eyes at her and merely sang another snatch of his song, becoming slightly incoherent.

Cat now noticed the boy, standing in the corner behind the door, looking at them from under his eyebrows with his head ducked down.

"Do you know what happened?" she asked him. He flinched, as if she had raised her hand to him, and then pointed at the table. On the heavy deal surface stood one of the brown pottery jugs they used to store Uncle's famous applejack. The stopper was loose, and a little of the potent liquor had spilled on the table. In the middle of the spill stood the turquoise Septimus cup.

"Look, Aunt!"

"Yes, child, I've seen." The older woman picked up the little tumbler and raised it to her nose. "That's what he drank from, I believe," she said, handing the cup to Cat and taking a sniff at the jug. "It's the brew we've had out for some weeks now; there's nothing wrong with it that I know."

Cat was cupping the vessel in both her hands and smelled the contents, then looked inside it. "No, there's nothing different about what was in here, but—Aunt. Try this." Cat gave the cup back to the wisewoman, who echoed her motion, wrapping both gnarly brown hands around the cup and taking a deep look inside the dish.

Ouska raised her head, and the two women exchanged a look.

"It's another enforcer," Cat said, "isn't it?"

"Yes, that's just what it is. Uncle here, he doesn't get drunk, and he often has a dram of his jack of an evening. He must have poured just one cup, and it's knocked him right back. Did he not?" Ouska asked the boy.

He flinched again as if struck, glowered at her from under his eyebrows, and then gave an infinitesimal nod.

"There you are, then," said Ouska. "The bowls, they give power to a person's wish to go to another place. These cups, it seems, give power to what's inside them; this one made the one small cup of applejack as potent as half a jug. Might be worth a try with mintbrew, or with some healing potions. But for now, help me get this old fool to his bed—he's going to have a head like a sore bear in the morning."

CHAPTER 9

"**Y**OU GOT POOR UNCLE drunk, you know," Cat said to her husband when she got home.

"What? What are you talking about?"

Cat was stashing her purchases in the lidded wooden shelf boxes they had taken to using to protect the food from the mouse plague. "The new Septimus cups! It appears they concentrate the powers of whatever is in them. Uncle poured a cup of applejack when he came home, and he ended up roaring drunk. Literally. By the time Aunt and I had him dragged to his bed, he was shouting at some imaginary foe about some imaginary insult. I've never heard anything like it. No wonder the boy was terrified—then again, somehow he looked like he was terrified on principle. He..."

"And you are talking of—what, exactly? Try to make sense, Madam Wife," said Guy, getting up from the bench and giving her a quick peck on the cheek as he leaned past her to snatch one of the apricot cakes back out of the box where Cat was trying to hide it. She swatted his fingers.

"They're for dessert! If you take yours now, I can't very well not give Bibby hers, too, can I!"

"Bibby 'ssert?" inquired a small voice behind them.

"There, see what you've done! No, Papa and Bibby get a cake *after* supper." She laughed at the identical pouts on their faces and firmly closed and latched the lid of the bread bin. "I was talking of the boy," she said to Guy, "your apprentice! Uncle brought him along. He'll be spending the night at their house; Aunt and I assumed there might still be a few things of his in the cart, and also, she said, if he's been apprenticed to Kaltbur and then handed over to Uncle, he's Uncle's responsibility until he can be properly brought to you. Sounds like indentured servitude to me, but, whatever. And so this kid jumped every time somebody spoke to him—well, every time either Aunt or I said something to him. We're not that terrifying, are we?"

"I won't answer that," said Guy with a grin. "I know what's good for me. So Uncle is bringing him tomorrow?"

"That's the plan—if Uncle can get his act together enough to do so. Where are we putting this kid to sleep? He's a teenager, not a small boy that can be tucked in the corner of the room—I was thinking in the workshop? If we put a pallet in the corner by the glazing shelves, that might work, don't you think?"

Uncle was indeed like a bear with a sore head when he came stomping through the woods the next morning, with the boy trailing after him carrying a small satchel. Not that Cat had ever encountered a sore-headed bear, but she could well imagine. Uncle's normally ruddy face was pale, and he was squinting his bleary, bloodshot eyes at even the filtered light falling through the forest leaves.

"Fool cup!" he muttered at his nephew. "How was I meant to know that was one of your fool creations, huh?" He squeezed the sides of his head with a groan.

"Well, the colour of the glaze might have given you an inkling," said Cat, a touch less sympathetic to his plight than she would have been had she not witnessed the ruckus he had made the night before. "Did you not see the travel bowls? They had the same glaze on them, and look what they managed to do."

"No, I didn't ever see the fool things," the older man mumbled through his beard. "The Woman might have said, but I had no call to be poking around the boy's workshop here to see what odd things he made with his odd fancies. And the Sepp took the last one. No, I never saw them," he grumbled.

"Well, no, I suppose you didn't, then," said Cat, "but it wasn't any of our fault. It wasn't anyone's fault, really, so you can stop grumbling at us. Is that all the luggage you brought?" she asked the boy, who flinched at her words.

"Yes, that's all he had," said Uncle, obviously making an effort to speak in less of a growl, but not succeeding very well. "Did you pack your boots in there, too?" he asked the boy, who nodded. *Interesting*, thought Cat. *He doesn't jump when Uncle talks to him. I wonder why.*

The teakettle was whistling on the stove, and Cat reached for it with a hot pad. She took out the brown round-bellied teapot; dropped in a small handful of mint leaves, dried yellow flowers, and some fine-needled herbs; and poured the boiling water on. From the shelf she took four brown-glazed mugs and one of the turquoise cups and brought them over to the table.

"Here, Uncle," she said, pouring the tea into the turquoise cup and holding it out to him, "try this."

He recoiled slightly. "Are you trying to poison me, girl?" he asked suspiciously.

"No, on the contrary," Cat said, pouring tea into the mugs and adding a shot of cold water to the one for Bibby, "I read in one of our books of herb lore at the library that mint with thyme and camomile is good for a headache. I'm sure Aunt would say the same. And if she and I are right about these cups..."

"Oh, very well," he grumbled, heavily sat down in the armchair at the end of the table, and reluctantly reached for the turquoise cup.

"Come on, Guy, and Bibby, and..." She looked at the boy. "We don't even know his name," she said to Uncle.

He paused with the cup halfway to his mouth, and looked surprised. "No more do I," he said, "I just got by with calling him boy, those two days on the road. We got along well enough, didn't we, boy." He got another slight nod in answer.

"Well, that won't do for us!" said Cat, frustrated. "We need to have a name for him!"

"What's your name, son?" asked Guy, laying a hand on the boy's shoulder. The youngster shied violently and knocked into Bibby, who had come up behind him. The little girl stumbled and clutched at the nearest object for support—the boy's trouser leg. His dark eyes opened wide in shock, and he froze. Bibby steadied herself on his leg, then reached out, grasped his hand, and wrapped her little fingers around it.

Cat found she was holding her breath.

The boy shuddered slightly, then turned his head and looked down into the little girl's wide turquoise eyes, turned up at him trustingly and a little quizzingly. The frightened look drained from his face.

"Andy!" said Bibby, and proudly looked around at her parents and uncle. The boy smiled at her, a very slight smile, but it nevertheless transformed his face into a look of singular sweetness.

"Andy?" asked Cat, "you think that's his name, Bibby?" The boy gave a slight shrug of his shoulder. "Very well," said Cat, with a feeling of profound relief, "Andy it is. Come over here, Andy, and have a cup of brew. You don't have a hangover, I assume, but it'll do you good nonetheless."

The boy sat down on one of the benches, and Cat put a mug of tea in front of him, which he took and gingerly began to sip at.

"Andy," said Guy, and gave the boy a steady look. "Well, do you think we can work together, son?"

He's stopped jumping, thought Cat. *Thank goodness for Bibby. Perhaps we can tame him yet.*

Uncle heaved a deep sigh. "That's better!" he said in his usual cheerful tone, putting the empty turquoise cup back on the table. His skin tone had returned to normal, and his eyes were clear. "The Woman, she's given me that brew before, when I were ill, but it never did its work as quick as that!"

"There, so perhaps those cups aren't fool pots, after all?" asked Cat with a smile.

"Well, no, not altogether," Uncle conceded. "But you better keep them out of the hands of fools!"

"We'll do that," promised Cat with a wink at him, "particularly when there is applejack anywhere nearby."

He threw her a look and hoisted himself to his feet.

"Very well, son," he said to Guy, "let's deal with those apprenticeship fees."

"Andy come," said Bibby, pulling on the boy's hand, "Andy yee bed!"

"Yes, you do that," said Cat, smiling at the little girl, "go take Andy to see his bed. You'll be sleeping in the workshop," she explained to him, and was glad to see he still didn't flinch. *Bless Bibby's little heart.* The boy gave a small nod and let himself be towed through the door into the workshop.

"That lad, there's something damned odd there," said Uncle quietly, when the boy and little girl were out of sight. "He stopped jumping at every word I said about an hour or so into our journey, once he saw I meant him no harm, and he was right handy with the horses. But never a word out of his mouth, and that look in his eyes... Kaltbur could make no headway with him. Now, that's as may be; your sister's man is not the right master for every apprentice there is. But after more than a month, you would expect something, now, wouldn't you? But nothing worked. The smile your babe got from him, that's the first I've ever seen out of the boy. Your mother found him fooling around with the mud in the back garden one day; that's what made them think of sending him out to work with you. So long as he stays with one of the family the contract is fulfilled."

"Who are his parents? Where did he hail from?" asked Guy with a frown.

"Who knows? Not from Ilim, he isn't. We'd have known. Your mother has many kin and friends in the city; one of them would have said. No, the fellow who brought him to be apprenticed, Kaltbur tells me, was an odd one—looked more like a rat than anything else, he said. Twitching nose and everything. Wasn't his father, nor yet a brother or uncle, Kaltbur thought."

"Wait," said Cat, "did he have black hair? And big ears? Did Kaltbur say?"

"Can't rightly say that he did—but no, he did say at that. No, not black—brown, grey-brown. That's what put Kaltbur in mind of a rat, hair that same colour as their mangy fur. And the teeth, he said, yellow and sticking out. Why?"

"There was someone in the market just like that, but with black hair, right when you and Andy came up the road. He was staring at me. And he reminded me of something, I couldn't think of what, but that's exactly it—he looked like a rat! A handsome rat, but still. Ugh. Well, he vanished. I hope that was the last I've seen of him; perhaps he came with the trader's caravan that brought Mother's letter and left with them again. Are you staying for a bite to eat, Uncle?"

"Thanks, girl, but I'd best get back to the Woman. I brought her some things from the city she'll want to take a look at, and I was in no frame to bring out trinkets this morning. Thanks for the potion! And you look after that boy—he needs it."

CHAPTER 10

*N*ICKY'S VOICE. *"BEN?"*

"Yeah? Over here, Nicky, I'm in my room."

"Ben, do you know someone called Tyrone Chilton?"

"No. Why?"

"Some guy by that name just called. He says he knows you, almost sounded like he was a relative of yours or something, and he wants to come visit. Are you sure you don't know him?"

"No. I mean, yes, I'm sure I never heard the name before."

"Okay, that weirds me out. He said he got my phone number from your old school. Why would they give out my phone number? Doesn't make sense. Hmm. If you say you don't know him, I'm glad I didn't agree to have him come here, that's for sure. I wonder if he can find out our address from the phone number?"

"I think it can be done—reverse lookup, or something."

"Well, my number is unlisted. So at least that shouldn't work. I told him I'd talk to you, and he should call back later."

The sound fading out. Silence.

Then the noise of the apartment door opening, fast steps receding down the hall, another door slamming. A pot lid clattering.

"Hi Sepp." Nicky's voice. "Oh, that smells good——what are you making, stew?"

"Yes. I came home a bit early from the job at your friend's; I thought I might as well start on supper. Where were you? And what is the matter with Ben?"

"You mean his running off to his room like that? Long story. Long, <u>weird</u> story, that. Could you put the kettle on? I need a cup of tea." The sound of water running, and the clicking of a kettle being put on a burner. Nicky's voice again. "So, yeah, as for where we were: we got this phone call earlier today, out of the blue, from some guy claiming to be a relative of Ben's, wanting to come visit—except Ben's never heard of him. He calls himself Tyrone, Tyrone Chilton. So, I mean, I'm not letting some stranger come here——"

"How did he get the phone number?"

The sound of a knife chopping vegetables.

"I have no idea! That's what creeps me out! Well, that was the first thing that creeped me out. So he was insisting he wanted to see 'little Benjamin', and I figured that if I didn't somehow agree to meet with him, he'd suddenly show up at the front door; he was that pushy. I thought maybe if we met him somewhere, he'd realize that he's got hold of the wrong kid and leave us alone. So I suggested meeting at a coffee shop—"

"Loulou's?"

"No, not Loulou's. That was my first thought too, but that's our special hangout—Lou knows me by name and

knows where I live; she might let something slip. I figured it'd be safer to go somewhere anonymous. So we went to the coffee place in the mall, that big one by the front entrance. I even parked a ways away, on the opposite side of the mall, so he wouldn't be able to follow us."

"You seem to be awfully cautious about this fellow."

"Well, yes—it might sound like I was being paranoid, but actually I'm wondering if I was paranoid enough! So we arranged to meet this guy at three-thirty at the Coffeebarn, right? I said three-thirty on purpose, because I knew we could get there early, so he wouldn't see us coming and figure out which was our car. We got there, got some drinks—did you know Ben drinks coffee? Straight up, black. He seems a bit young for that much caffeine—makes me wonder about that mother of his; what kind of habits did she teach that kid? And speaking of his mom..."

"One thing at a time. And yes, I knew about his coffee drinking. I'm home more than you, remember. Sometimes he loads it up with about five spoons of sugar, too, but never any milk like you do. So you got drinks, and then?"

"And then we just sat at a table and waited. So Ben's chattering on at me—you know how he gets—"

"Yes, I know. He's been quite talkative lately, hasn't he? And cheerful. Rather amazing for losing his parents only a month ago."

"Yeah, exactly! So, anyway, Ben's telling me about this TV show you guys keep watching, jabber jabber jabber, and all of a sudden he clams up. Bam. In the middle of a sentence. Claps his mouth shut, and gets this look on his face... Sepp, I tell you, I was scared. I've never seen him look that way *before; he looked terrified. And what it was—he'd caught sight of this Tyrone guy. Now, Ben said he didn't know him, but he must have. Not only did he react to this guy, but the guy came right over to our table; he recognized Ben all right. And, Sepp—ugh! That guy gives me the willies, he looks like a freakin' rat! Huge nose, receding forehead and chin, and his hair is this ratty dirty greyish colour. Not really grey from old age—he's probably no more than thirty-five, forty—but, I don't know, just not really brown. And then his teeth—"*

"So what was Ben doing all this time?"

"Sitting there, staring at the table in front of him. I was trying to be polite, doing the introduction thing and all. So this guy is doing this smarmy act—probably was trying to be charming, or something; it so wasn't working. His grin—ugh! His teeth are all yellow, and the two front ones are really narrow, with a big overbite—I tell you, exactly like a rat! So he sits down beside Ben and starts talking about how they used to be such good friends, and he said something about Ben's 'dear mother'. That's the only time Ben opened his mouth, and I could have sworn he said 'Not my mother!' It was hard to hear, though, it's almost like he was choking when he said it, he could hardly get the words out. And then this guy grabs him by the arm, still doing this repulsive fake-friendship act—but he got a real grip on Ben, digging his claws right into the kid's biceps. Ben kind of freaked out and tore his arm away and knocked over his coffee, right into my lap. Well, so I accidentally-on-purpose knocked mine over onto Ben—pretending he made me jump, you know—and it gave us the excuse to get out of there in a hurry. I told the Tyrone guy we had to go clean up, and

it'd been nice meeting him. I haven't told that fat a lie in a while! We hightailed to the washrooms by the drugstore; they have an outside exit to the parking lot. I think we gave that guy the slip. I hope he's still sitting in the Coffeebarn growing mould, waiting for us to come back!"

"And Ben?"

"Ben didn't say a word the whole way back. I tried asking him, wondered if he was really sure he didn't know this guy before, but he was just shaking his head——and then he got something almost like an asthma attack, so I just shut up and got him home. He seemed okay by the time we got here, and I think he just needs some time to get over it. Sepp, I wonder if this has anything to do with Charlie and his drug buddies. Rat-face Tyrone, I wouldn't put it past him; he's exactly the sort of creep Charlie used to hang out with. There's something weird about this guy's eyes—they're not quite druggie pinpoint pupils, but something isn't right. They're too round, or too black, or something—I can't put my finger on it..."

A saucepan lid clattering.

Sepp's voice. "Well, here, have a taste of this. Maybe you can put your finger on what's wrong with it. It's got carrots, potatoes, the meat from yesterday, some tomatoes, and your friend gave me some parsley she had growing on the windowsill."

"Well, Marlene isn't exactly a friend—coworker, really. Mmm, that's good, nothing wrong with it. Just maybe a little more salt? But not much. So, I don't know what to do about rat face—maybe he'll just leave us alone. Here's hoping."

"We can only wait and see, and be careful in the meantime. There, how's this?" The sound of a spoon clinking against a pot rim.

Nicky's voice. "Yeah, that did the job, that's enough salt. Oh, and there's some green onions left in the bottom of the fridge, they could be good. So the job at Marlene's went well? She sure liked that cupboard door you did for her last week."

"Yes, that turned out well. Today's job, too. Those power tools you have here make for so much faster work. My brace at home isn't nearly as quick."

"Brace? Oh, that's a hand-powered drill, isn't it?"

"Yes. I was quite proud of it, because it's such an improvement on the bow drill I started with, but it's nothing like a power drill. But there is still something to be said for doing things by hand. Speaking of which, pass me the cutting board, please?"

"Uh, yeah, you scare me with your vegetable chopping speed! Stop grinning, it's not funny! One of these days—watch it! You almost took your fingertip off there!"

"Did not. Scaredy cat."

"I'm not Cat!"

"Fine, scaredy mouse then."

"Ugh! Don't even say that word!"

Ben's voice. "What are you guys fighting about?"

"Your aunt, Young Ben, won't trust me to handle a large, sharp knife safely. What she doesn't seem to understand is that people who have used hand tools all their lives get really good at it. See?"

Ben's voice, enthusiastic. "Oh, sweet! Like those sword dances you see on TV! Can you show me how to do that?"

78

"No, he damn well cannot!" Nicky's voice, sounding outraged. "He's <u>not</u> teaching you to twirl that knife around in circles so you can take everyone's fingers off, it's freakin' sharp!"

Sepp's voice. "It had better be. A sharp tool is a safe tool. Remember that, Ben."

"Yes, Master Yoda. When's that stew done? I'm starving, Nicky."

"Then go and take the soup bowls into the living room—oh, don't forget the spoons. Here." Dishes rattling, then Nicky's voice, quietly: "He seems to have gotten over it—thank goodness. Help me keep an eye on him, Sepp? Please?"

"Of course I will, dear. Don't worry; he's got both of us to look out for him. We're not letting anyone at him. It's all right, Nicky, it will be all right."

A sniff.

"I'm so glad you're here, Sepp..."

CHAPTER 11

T HE BLACK WALNUTS IN the little garden behind the library had fully ripened and dropped off the trees, and Nikor Archivist declared it was time to make ink. He was completely uninterested in the nuts themselves; all he wanted were the black husks, papery and a little crumbly like the humus of the ground they would soon turn into. Cat, however, wanted the nuts; she remembered a nut cake her grandmother used to make that had been one of her favourites. Maybe she could find a way to replicate that recipe, or ask Guy's cousin if she had one; Yldra was a fantastic pastry baker. From what Cat remembered, her grandmother's walnut pastry had been fairly plain—just a cake with lots of chopped nuts on it. She began gathering the large walnuts, some of them as big as a small chicken's egg, into the leather scrip strapped around her waist.

"You don't mind my taking the nuts, do you?" she asked Nikor, who was busy gathering the husks into a large cast iron pot.

"Nuts? Nuts. Oh no, no no. Take the nuts, make the husks easier to find."

Cat dropped a handful of the black husks into his pot.

"Too bad the pot is so rusty," she said. "Won't that harm the ink?"

"No, no no. Rust is good, makes blacker ink. New pots are no good for ink. Besides, ink spoils the pots, makes stains."

"Well, yes, I suppose it would—it's ink, after all, it's supposed to stain. So how do we do this?"

They carried the pot, now half filled with the black walnut husks, into Nikor's living space in the back room of the library.

"Stinks, does ink," said Nikor, "but don't want to make a fire outside now. Prefer my stove." He filled the pot with enough water to cover the husks and put it on top of the little potbellied stove in the corner of his room, which already had a nice little fire crackling in it. "Spoon, spoon—where's the spoon?" he muttered, digging around in a box of cooking implements that stood on a shelf above the wood box.

"You mean this one?" said Cat, extracting a wooden spoon from between several stacks of books on the floor beside a worn leather-covered armchair. The spoon's bowl was stained a deep mahogany colour, in contrast to the blonde wood of its handle. "What's it doing between the books?"

"Books? Oh, yes. Mouse, hit at the mouse with it when I was reading. See, ink stains," he explained, pointing to the discolouration of the spoon.

"Oh, that's from ink?" Cat said distractedly, not listening to his answer. The top book of one of the stacks had caught her attention. Covered in brown leather, it had an image of a rat-like creature stamped on it, and the title proclaimed it *The Rats of Chaelia*. Cat was intrigued. She picked up the book, sat down in Nikor's chair, and got lost in the story. It seemed to be from many centuries ago, telling of two tribes of people, one called the Grey Rats, the other the Black, locked in a generations-old struggle for supremacy. Each group had its heroes and its legends; they reminded Cat of *The Iliad* with its battle for Troy. Back and forth the fight went between the two factions; one time the Greys were on the top, then the Blacks won the battle and had their contender on the throne, and then it all went back again. Each side was absolutely convinced that they were the rightful rulers of their country, Chaelia.

"Where is Chaelia?" she asked Nikor, raising her head to find that the room was much darker than it had been when they brought in the nuts. Nikor was nowhere in sight, and a frightful stink rose from the steaming pot on the stove. Cat felt disoriented. Hadn't she only just sat down? It could hardly have been more than a few minutes ago, could it? She stood and took a look at the stinking pot. In the bottom of the container, a dark sludge was bubbling away. The walnut husks had mostly disintegrated into smaller pieces now, making the whole mess a deep, brownish black. Cat wrinkled her nose—the stench was quite pronounced, metallic and rotten at the same time.

The door from the main library room creaked open, and Nikor shuffled back into the room, carrying two more books.

"Found it, found it," he said, dumping the books into Cat's arms and picking up the wooden spoon to poke at the black sludge in the pot. "Ah yes, coming along nicely."

"Found what?" Cat asked.

"Looking for the books of Chaelia, wasn't I," he said. He waved a finger at the book Cat had been reading. "*The Rats* is just one; there are others."

"Just where is Chaelia? Is it one of the places in Isachang?" Cat asked.

"No, no no. Chaelia is Outland, don't you know?"

"Outland? *My* Outland, where I'm from? You mean Earth, or America, or whatever?"

"Yes. No. No no. Not Arthur Pendragon. Other land, other Outland. There are many. Haven't seen anyone from Outlands here in generations, many many generations, not since Septimissimus last."

"There are other Outlands? Really? And—what did you just say, about the Septimissimus?"

"Septimissimus?" he repeated, stirring the ink sludge in the bottom of the pot. He pulled out a spoonful and dribbled a bit on a piece of paper. "Not dark enough yet, more hours," he muttered. "Septimissimus? Yes. Last Septimissimus, seventh son of seventh son of Septimus family, seven hundred years ago. A coming and going between Isachang and Outworlds, brought books, brought tales; people came and went and stayed."

"So that's why—" Cat began, tipping her head sideways and thinking, "that's why I was able to come across!"

"What? No Septimissimus now, is there?"

"Of course there is," Cat said, "Guy—Dyniselm, my husband, don't you remember? Everyone thought it was Sepp—Risyl, I suppose you called him when you were teaching them their letters—but it wasn't—isn't. You know!"

"Oh. Oh yes, yes." He scratched at his white hair fringe with the handle of the spoon. "Septimus sons, yes. Get old, forget things. Put it in a book, I remember. People——change, move, grow. Young Dyniselm, now—forgot he was grown, for a moment."

"It's okay," said Cat, smiling affectionately at the little librarian. "We're making new ink, we'll write it all down soon, then you won't forget. So is this all we do with the ink, boil it?"

"Yes, boil it and boil it. Then strain it, and bottle it, and write with it, that's what we do with ink." He gave a wheezy little chortle at his own witticism. Cat grinned. Nikor was quite a character.

"Nikor, I should go. I had no idea it was getting so late. I'm going by Yldra's; I think the kittens will soon be old enough to go home. Do you want me to pick one out for the library?"

"Kitten? Small cat. Ah yes, yes. Do, do. Good night, Catriona Bookwoman. Take tales of Chaelia, bring back next time. Good night."

~~ele~~

When Cat got to Yldra's house, she found Guy there, perched at the bench by the kitchen table, sipping a cup of peppermint tea—mintbrew, they called it—and chin-wagging with his cousin and her husband. Cat smiled at them all in turn and gave Guy a quick kiss as she leaned over the table, drawing her sleeve across the surface to wipe up a slight dribble from his cup—she couldn't put the books down on a damp spot, that would never do.

"More books?" Guy shook his head at her. "There is no more room on the mantel!"

"Don't worry, I'm taking them back soon."

"That's what you said last time! There are still at least half a dozen there!" He wrinkled his nose. "And what's more, you stink. Of ink. You and yon little wizard have been brewing potions, haven't you? I remember how the whole library stank when he boiled ink while we had lessons."

"Yes, we've been brewing walnut potions to weave spells on paper. You're right; it smells awful. And, oh, look!" She opened her scrip and showed her hoard of round, shiny nuts. "I've been squirrelling!" She stuck out her front teeth over her bottom lip like a rodent and twitched her nose.

"Ooh, don't!" Yldra shuddered. "You look like a mouse when you do that, and I can't bear the sight or thought of those creatures anymore! Food spoiled, storage gnawed on, mouse dirt in the cupboards... it's awful!"

"Oh yes," said Cat, "that reminds me: I'm commissioned to choose Ruph's new town library cat. You know Nikor; he never leaves the library, so the cat must be brought to him. The kittens are almost ready to go, aren't they?"

"They are. Why don't you go see them? They're in the shed; the children are probably out there playing with them anyhow. You go ahead, I just need to get the scrap bucket for the chickens."

Guy drained the last bit of his mintbrew and got up to follow Cat to the small lean-to stable where Yldra kept her goat and chickens. Little Bibby and Yldra's boy Randor, a year or so older than Bibby, were busy tumbling about in the small hayloft.

"Bubba!" squealed Bibby, launching herself at her dad, who caught her just in time. "Bubba, kiki!"

"Yes, dear, kitty. Where are they? Mama wants to choose one for the library." He picked straw out of his little daughter's red-gold curls.

"Libwy kiki?"

"Yes, a kitty for the library," said Guy, putting the little girl back on the ground.

"Bibby kiki too!"

"No, sweetie," said Cat, "you know we can't have one of Aunty Yldra's kitties. They've all got homes to go to already. Remember? There are so many mice, people need lots of kitties."

The corners of Bibby's little mouth turned down, and her bottom lip started to wobble.

"Bibby wan' kiki!"

"Oh dear, you've had a long and tiring day, haven't you," said Cat. "I think maybe we'd best go home; I can pick out Nikor's cat some other day."

"*Bibby kiki!*" whined the little girl, and stomped her feet. Guy scooped her up.

"Now that's enough," he said firmly, "you heard what Mama said."

Bibby howled. "KIKI!!"

"What's the matter?" asked Yldra, who had come into the shed behind them with her bucket of chicken feed.

"Oh, Bibby's just overtired," said Cat, "she's making a fuss because I told her she can't have one of the kittens—they're all spoken for, aren't they?"

"Well, yes, these ones are," said Yldra, "but our Greyface just had a litter, too, a few days ago. I haven't let the children at them, as the kittens are too young yet to be handled much, and if the little ones knew they were there they would not have left them alone; but there's five of them, you can have one of those."

Bibby gave a little hiccoughing sob. "Kiki?" she asked, her large turquoise eyes swimming with tears. Guy and Cat looked at each other.

"Well, why not?" said Guy.

"It would be great," said Cat to Yldra. "We really do need a cat."

"Very well, then," said Yldra in her mother's no-nonsense tone, "why don't you come and see them. It'll make the little one happy to know that she's got a kitten to look forward to, so she's not fussing all night long. She's fully capable of it, I know, with that stubborn streak of hers—who knows where she gets that from." She quirked up her eyebrow at Guy, who just snorted. Yldra took her little son's hand and led the way to a corner of the shed, where a wooden board was leaning at an angle against the wall. She peered behind it. "We're in luck, Greyface just stepped out," she said, and carefully pulled aside the board. Behind it, nestled in a box padded with some old rags, lay a litter of tiny kittens. Two were black, two were brown tabbies, and the last one was a beautiful silver-grey.

"Kitties!" squealed the children, and tried to swoop on the little creatures.

"No, dears, you have to be very gentle!" Yldra said, holding them back. "The kitties are very tiny. Sit down, and I'll take one out for each of you." Little Randor and Bibby plopped down on the floor of the shed and expectantly held out their hands. Yldra lifted one of the black kittens, which was nestled against its grey sibling, and placed it in her son's lap.

"Dat one!" said Bibby, pointing at the grey kitten.

"I don't know, dear," said Yldra, "that kitty has something wrong with its foot."

"Dat one!" insisted Bibby. Her aunt picked up the kitten, and Cat saw that there was indeed something badly wrong with the kitten. Its right back leg was a short, bloody stump, looking sore and inflamed. Bibby held out her hands.

"Bibby kiki!" she demanded; so Yldra laid the kitten gently in her hands.

"Careful now with it, very careful." She turned to Guy and Cat. "The little thing had its birth cord wrapped around its leg when it was born——or for some time before that, I suspect; it cut off the leg."

The kitten mewed, crying with soft chirping noises. Bibby looked down at the tiny cat, her eyes big in her little face. Suddenly she thrust the kitten out to Guy.

"Kiki owie! Bubba make better. New foot!"

Guy and Cat looked at each other, startled. When had Bibby learned that her father could sometimes cure an injury merely by touching it? He'd only found out very recently himself. Unfortunately, it had only rarely worked, just twice so far that Cat knew of, and only when he had caused the hurt himself, albeit accidentally. One of those occasions had been her own hand.

"I'm sorry, dear," Guy said, regretfully, "I don't think I can make the kitten better."

Bibby's bottom lip started to wobble again.

"Bubba make better!" She insistently held the kitten out to Guy. It meeped pitifully.

"Well, I can't make it worse," said Guy with a compassionate look at Bibby and gently took the little animal from her hands. It lay curled up on his palm, crying. He cupped the long, slender fingers of his other hand over the kitten, and a look of intense concentration came over his face. The kitten's crying suddenly stopped, and the look on Guy's face changed to one of startled surprise.

"I think he just started purring!" he said, lifting his fingers to look at the kitten curled up on his hand. It was kneading his palm with its front paws and was nuzzling around, obviously looking for a nipple. Guy stroked the kitten with one finger, and then lifted up the little leg stump. "Look! Not a new leg, but it seems like the end is healed up!" He held out the kitten for Cat and Yldra to see.

"Well done, dear," said Cat, smiling proudly at him.

"Thank you—but I don't know what I did," he said. "It just happened. Even though I had nothing to do with the hurt at first. Hmm..."

"Kiki?" said Bibby, standing on tiptoe to see on her father's hand.

"Yes, look, Bibby," said Guy, "kitty is feeling better now!" He made her sit on the floor again and placed the kitten back in her hands. She gave the kitten a little kiss and gently held it to her chest.

"Bibby kiki!" she said, as if it was a settled matter.

Cat laughed. "I guess we just adopted a defective kitten!" she said. "Do you suppose he'll be able to walk?"

"Oh, probably," said Yldra. "It was that sore, the infection, that had me worried; I've seen three-legged cats before. Do you remember," she said to Guy, "Aegar at the inn had a three-legged ginger tom for years when we were children. He was the terror of all the other cats in the neighbourhood."

"Bewarrre the three-legged cat!" said Cat in a mock-piratical voice. "Oh, I know! We can call him Long John Silver!"

Guy and Yldra looked at her.

"Oh, it's a story we have in my world, of a boy who goes hunting for treasure on an island; it has a wicked one-legged pirate in it by the name of Long John Silver. You know, 'Bewarrre the one-legged man,' that sort of thing. Would fit, wouldn't it? Three-legged cat? Silver coat? Long John Silver?"

Guy grinned his lopsided grin at her. "Whatever you like, Madam Wife. We can call the cat Long John Silver if it makes you happy. But you'll have to tell us the whole story of the treasure island some evening."

"Look, Bibby," said Cat, "here's mama cat come back. We need to put little Johnny back in the nest so he can have some milk."

"Dzonny milk," said Bibby willingly and let Cat take the kitten from her hands to put him back in the box. "Den Bibby and Dzonny go home?"

"No, not yet, dear," said Yldra. "You don't have milk for kitty, he needs to stay with his mama until he's bigger. But then he can come live with you, all right? Perhaps a few weeks before winter solstice." She took the black kitten that little Randor had been cuddling and put it to nurse next to its grey brother. "Say good night to the kittens now."

"Goo' nigh' kiki," echoed the little girl, "Bibby come back soon!" She let her father carry her out of the shed into the quickly falling dusk.

CHAPTER 12

Sepp's voice. "Ben, did you know it's Nicky's birthday today?"

"No, I had no idea! Dang, I don't have anything to give her for a birthday present. I'd like to give her something, you know? She gave me that cool Swiss army knife for mine. We could go get her something before she gets home from work, the mall's still open. But I don't have any cash or anything, can you spot me some?"

"I'm afraid not; the wage for my last job went for buying food. I don't know what to give her either. We still have a bit of time, though; do you think she might like having a cake baked?"

"Yeah, probably—you make good cakes. Chocolate—make her a chocolate cake, she'll like that."

"You mean <u>you</u> will like that, you greedy little..."

The sounds of a scuffle, then Ben's voice, breathless and laughing. "Uncle, uncle!"

"I'm not your uncle, boy, stop trying to turn me up sweet!"

"That means you're supposed to let me go; I give up, man! Oof, get off me!" A chuckle from Sepp, and shuffling sounds. Ben's voice. "But honest, I think Nicky likes chocolate cake!"

"Very well, I'll see what I can do." Sounds of cupboard doors opening. "Hey, Ben, why don't you give her the owl?"

Ben's voice, gruff. "What, the one I made? Nah. It's stupid. I was just fooling around. It's no good."

Sepp's voice. "Yes, it is, Ben. I've told you, it's a really good piece of carving. You have a knack for woodworking. Go ahead, why don't you?"

"Nah, I told you. She'd just hate it. She wouldn't want something that I made."

"Ben... why would you think that?"

Ben's voice, quiet, constricted. "I know women. They don't want some stupid thing some stupid kid made; she'd probably just throw it out."

"Son, we're talking about Nicky here. Do you really think she would be so mean?"

"I tell you, I know about women. I don't want to give her the stupid owl. I'll just help you with the cake."

Sepp's voice with an amused undertone. "Licking the bowl isn't helping." Then serious. "But I'll make you a deal: you can help with the cake, and it can be a gift from both of us, if you give her the owl, too."

The sounds of clattering dishes fading.

A door clicking open.

Nicky's voice. "Something smells awfully good in here!"

"Surprise!" "Happy Birthday!"

"Oh! How did you find out it was my birthday today?"

"Sepp said."

"I saw your old membership card for the reenactors lying around. It had your birthday on it." Sepp's voice. "The kid says you like chocolate cake—was he right, or were there ulterior motives at work here?"

"Both, I guess. I do like chocolate—who doesn't? Yum. Oh, what's this? A present? Neat!"

Paper rustling.

Nicky's voice, enthusiastic. "Oh, this is cute! And I love the colour of the wood. Where did you get that? The gift shop in the mall? What? What's with the significant look, Sepp? Did Ben pick it out?"

"He didn't <u>pick it out</u>, no..."

Ben's voice, panicked. "Don't tell her! That wasn't part of the deal!"

"What?" Nicky's voice. "Tell me what? What deal? Hey, what's that carved on the bottom? Looks like BB."

Sepp's chuckle. "It's the carver's mark——the initials."

Ben, shouting. "Don't tell!!"

"The carver's mark? What? Oh—BB—not Ben Bauer? Ben, no way—you didn't make that yourself, did you?"

"Come on, speak up, young Ben, admit it."

Ben's voice, very quiet, gruff. "Fine. Yeah, I made it. I know it's stupid."

"Stupid?!? It's gorgeous! I liked it when I thought it was bought, but if you <u>made</u> that... Wow! When, how?"

Sepp's voice. "In the basement, mostly with his Swiss army knife. He saw me whittling around on a piece of scrap wood I brought from that job at Marlene's, and he wanted to try. Nicky, he's a natural! I'm not bad with wood, but I've been doing this since I was little. That owl is his first piece of carving, and..."

"Why are you shaking your head, Ben? It's not your first?"

Ben's voice very, very quiet, nearly choking. "No... Mad e... a bird... once..."

"Your mother." Sepp's voice. "That's why you didn't want to give this to Nicky—your mother threw out the bird you made."

"She's... not... my... mother!!" Coughing, choking.

"Whoa, easy, son, take it easy! Deep breath, Ben—breathe, damn you, breathe! There—another breath—come on—another one—good. Nice deep breaths." The sound of a tap running. "Here, drink this—it's just water, you need it. Come on, down the hatch with it. There, that's better. Whoa. What was that about? Look at Nicky, she's white as a sheet; you gave her a big fright."

Nicky's voice, scared. "Yes, you did, Ben! Don't <u>do</u> that sort of thing!" More calmly. "Look, I know there's some stuff behind all this, but if it's bothering you that much, you don't need to talk about it, okay? We can figure it out slowly, one step at a time. And you know what, Ben, I have to hug you—sorry about that, but I do—for not dying in front of my eyes, for one, and for giving me that beautiful owl..."

Sepp's voice. "Do I get a hug, too? I made you a cake!"

"Oh, fine. And you saved my favourite nephew from choking. I guess you deserve a hug..."

Ben's voice. "Ahem! Teenager in the room! You can let go of each other now, you're embarrassing me! Oooh, Nicky's blushing, Nicky's blushing!"

Sepp's voice. "Someone recovered a little too quickly from his choking fit, I think!"

"Hah, you're blushing, too-hoo! Ouch!! No giving noogies, ouch!" The sound of a scuffle.

"Stop it, boys! No roughhousing in the living room! Cut it out, or I'm not sharing my cake! There, owl goes on the mantelpiece. Right next to your bowl, Sepp. Doesn't he look great there? Let's make some coffee to go with the cake."

Cat slowly surfaced from sleep. The dreams were getting more and more vivid, and she was sure she was hearing them closer to the time they actually happened. October thirtieth, Nicky's birthday. That was today. Nicky was turning twenty-seven, and Cat wasn't there to celebrate. She missed her friend. But somehow—somehow she thought she'd be seeing her again soon. It sounded like Sepp was making inroads. And Ben—she remembered Nicky mentioning him once.

It's probably around six o'clock, or a bit later, thought Cat. Dawn was slowly creeping in through the window above their box bed. She snuggled deeper under the covers. The bed had been a surprise from Guy, just a few days after Andy had come to live with them. Cat smiled. She would not have thought that sleeping in what amounted to a wardrobe would be so amazingly cozy—a very deep wardrobe without a back that was standing right up against the window. Getting into bed was like being in a really tiny bedroom with a five-foot ceiling where the mattress and bedding took up all of the floor space. It reminded Cat of some pictures she had seen of Japanese capsule hotels where each room was a sort of pod that people crawled into at night.

Cat loved having her own space where she could close the doors and be alone for a bit, and even have some privacy for herself and her husband at night. Living in a one-room cottage had been a novelty at first, and she had found ways to get time to herself, off and on, but with the colder fall weather setting in, her refuge in the forest was becoming less and less appealing. And now that Andy was living with them, there was no place to be really private. She had been grumbling to Guy about it on one of the days when Bibby had been fussing a lot, tracked dirt in the house, spilled food on the floor, and then thrown a tantrum about not being able to go visit the kitten, and Cat had felt extra tired from having spent most of the previous day in the library helping Nikor sort the books into a semblance of Dewey Decimal order. All she had wanted that day was to retreat, to be alone, so she could bury her head in her book without having Bibby tug on her sleeve every other minute demanding attention, wanting to be told a story or telling one herself. Cat loved her stepdaughter and was more than happy to be a mum, but there were days when she simply wanted a door to close on people. And the next day Guy had got her one. Apparently the furniture maker in the village had had the pieces of the bed mostly assembled in his shop for a while—someone in Kashinka's family had commissioned it and then changed their mind, because the design was not fancy enough for them. Cat was glad; she much preferred plain designs to ornate ones. The only elaborate piece of furniture they owned was the beautiful rocking chair Sepp had made when Bibby was born; the box bed was made on much simpler lines, practical rather than elegant.

She let the dream play in her head again. Sepp. So he was teaching Nicky's ward to carve wood. Interesting. It sounded like they had a good relationship going there. And Sepp, cheerful and easy-going, would be a great match for her best friend, just as his brother's intensity was a good balance to Cat's own commonsensical approach to life. Guy's tendency towards histrionics seemed to have toned itself down lately, though; in fact, if Cat had not seen that he could occasionally flare up with the power of an explosion, she would never have known he had a temper now.

Cat stretched and bumped into the side of the bed. The cupboard doors swung open a little, and she could hear Bibby's soft breathing from her little trundle bed that pulled out from underneath the box bed on the side. Most nights, the little girl still crawled into bed with them sometime during the night; Guy had apparently put her back into her own bed in the small hours.

Cat heard scrabbling in the kitchen corner. Those dratted mice! She had taken to hanging her pots and pans on hooks suspended from the ceiling, because otherwise she had to clean mouse dirt out of each dish every time before using it. Disgusting. She could hardly wait until they got the cat—although she supposed it would be some time before three-legged little Johnny would be able to do any mousing. But then, she had heard that just having a cat in the house would help the situation; the theory was that the mice would smell the cat and stay away. One could but hope. Meanwhile, there were traps. A snap and an abruptly terminated squeak told her that one had just claimed another victim. Hah, take that, vermin!

She cautiously slid out from under the covers, climbed out of the bed, and tiptoed over to the fireplace. On the mantel above the water heater was her stack of books. She had taken out the tale of the Grey and Black Rats of Chaelia again; there was something that fascinated her about that story. She took the book, wrapped herself in a shawl, and settled into the rocking chair by the front window. There was just enough light coming in to read by.

CHAPTER 13

*T*HE SOUND OF VOICES *as if from a distance away, like a radio playing in the next room.*

A woman's voice, commanding, sharp. "Have you found them yet?"

A cringing, servile male voice. "No, my lady, not—not yet. But I come closer. The oracle becomes more clear."

"Well, get on, make haste! We have need for them; you know full well we have need. The glories of the throne must be restored!"

"Yes, my lady."

"What happened to the other one, the one we sent away a double sevennight ago?"

"I know not, my lady. He took the stones, which the portent told us were the key, and was taken of a sudden; he has not been seen by a soul since that very hour. Yet the portent tells me he has found the hiding place to which the grey one, curse his soul, has taken the young slave. We shall find the young slave, my lady, find him and take him, and make his gift serve our ends; my lady, we shall find him and thwart the aimings of the grey ones, curse their souls. They sought to

hinder us, they sought to remove the slave from our powers, but we shall find him, and we shall..."

"Silence! Very well. Keep seeking through the portents. But be minded, we must needs have them both; one alone will not serve. The glories of the throne must be restored!"

The sound crackling, the voices fading out, overlaid by a stronger, more effective signal.

Sepp's voice. "Nicky? What's the matter?"

"It was that rat guy again, the Tyrone fellow. Sepp, I'm scared..."

"It's all right, dear, it's all right. Come here, come. So what is it? Tell me, dear. Come, no need to cry. It'll be all right. What happened?"

The sound of Nicky sniffling, blowing her nose.

"Thanks... It just freaks me out so bad... Ben was so upset when he got home from school, chalk white, but he couldn't even talk about it—you know how he gets. He was just about hyperventilating when he walked in. He'd been running from this guy, dodging him—oh Sepp, I hope to God he didn't see where Ben was going. If he knew where we live... And when I asked Ben what was the matter and he tried to answer, he started choking. It's that choking and coughing again, I can't stand it, Sepp! I finally figured it out, and asked Ben outright so he didn't have to say anything—if all he has to do is nod or shake his head, it's not so bad, but it's like he can't talk about this, about rat guy, about Verena, anything like that; he just can't get the words out. It turns out the guy has been hanging around outside the school; Ben's been ducking out the back door to try to avoid him, but today

he thought he was spotted. I'm surprised the school hasn't called in the cops yet; they're usually super quick about that."

"Hmm. They might not know he's there. There could be something that's preventing them from seeing him. There is something about him..."

"What? What do you mean? And, wait—have you actually seen him? Has he ever seen you?"

"Yes, I saw him once on the street, I knew him from your description, but I don't believe he knows me yet, or that I belong with you. There is something odd about him, something I recognize."

"Well, he totally looks like a rat! It's gross..."

"No, I don't mean how he looks. There is a feeling about him, some power or force. I saw it once before, in Ruph, when I was young—it was a trader merchant at the solstice fair who sold medicines, or so he claimed. He tried to sell me on a bottle of potion; he said would make me run faster and be stronger than all the other boys—well, the sort of thing that appeals to a child of ten. I was the only one at that stall, as if nobody else saw this trader but me, and something reeled me in. It's like he wanted to gain some power over me, get a hold of me for some purpose, and it wasn't a friendly one. But my father came along just in time and noticed what was going on; I never saw him angrier in my life, ever. Father had a temper, just like Guy does, but that time he just went extremely quiet. He told me to run along, and usually I would have balked, but I was only too glad then—that trader somehow frightened me, and Father's eyes were—well, not like anything I have seen before or since. And the next day that stall was gone from the fair. This rat fellow, he has the

same feel around the edges as that trader had. Not nearly as strong, but it's there. I think this world dampens a lot of these kinds of powers, or forces..."

"Sepp, darlin', don't. You know I don't like it when you talk like that—this talk of being from another world..."

Sepp's voice, quietly. "Nicky, it's true. You need to come to terms with it—it's the truth. I know it's hard, but try, dear, please. I have a feeling that soon, it'll be very important that you do. Just try. Give it—how do you always put that—the doubt of the benefit."

"Benefit of the doubt. Okay, I'll try, just to make you happy. But don't blame me if I don't totally succeed." Sounds of dishes clattering. Nicky's voice. "Do you want a cup of tea? I'm making Earl Grey. Okay. Well, it's just hard to get a handle on all this, you know? But, to be honest, with this creepy Tyrone guy—you're right, there's something about him that's not quite right. It's like he's blurry around the edges, but still somehow, I dunno, scary. Menacing, that's how he comes across, and not in any way that I've ever felt before. And believe me, I've met menacing before; some of Charlie's so-called friends were... ugh. But with this guy, it's worse because he was acting so smarmy, pretending really hard to be a nice guy, but underneath he frightens me. Well, he frightens _me_; he _terrifies_ Ben. Whatever went on between them, it must have been bad, really traumatic for Ben. I don't know what to do, Sepp..."

"It seems to me that it would be best if we tried to keep Ben out of his reach, made sure he doesn't go back to the places where this fellow expects him to be."

"That would mean taking him out of school, wouldn't it?"

"Yes, if that's possible, that would be best, I think."

"Well, that makes sense. I suppose I could just call the school and tell them Ben is sick—or better yet, I'll tell them that he's come out with some allergic reaction to something in the school building, or is having stress breakdowns because of the car accident, and that we'll homeschool him until further notice. I think that could work, then they won't ask too many questions. Here's your tea. Do you want milk and sugar? Or is this one of your no-milk days? You know, usually people take it one way or the other; they don't keep changing their minds about it. And could you be a darlin', darlin', and take this one to Ben? He's probably buried in a comic book trying to make himself feel better, but I think it'll do him good if you check on him and make sure he's okay. See if he's breathing."

"All right, give it here."

The clinking of a spoon against a cup, then the sound of a kiss.

Sepp's voice. "What was that for?"

"What? Oh, nothing. I'm just so glad you're here, Sepp. God, I'm so glad you're here... I don't think we could cope without you..."

"Nicky! Dear! What did I say about crying? Come here, you. It's all right. I promise, it'll be all right... Come on, let's both of us take Ben his tea, okay?"

Nicky's voice muffled. "No, you go ahead." Then clearer, "I'm calling the school. And you know what," a sniff, "I'm getting really pissed off. This Tyrone creep is messing up my life, mine and my kid's and my boyfriend's..."

"Hey, am I your boyfriend? That's good to know."

"Well, yeah. You've been living with me for two months, I think that qualifies, don't you?"

"Yes, I suppose it does... Although doesn't this boyfriend-girlfriend thing mean a bit more than just, well, me sleeping on your couch?"

"Darn, well, yeah. I was hoping you hadn't figured that out... The tea is getting cold. And if I don't call the school right now, the secretary will have gone home. Go on, shoo!"

Cat's eyes flew open, and she looked around, feeling disoriented. It was broad daylight in the room. Daylight? Why was she sleeping in the daytime? Then she remembered—she'd been feeling terribly tired all morning, and lay down for just a minute while Bibby was having her nap. She had a feeling that that had been more than an hour ago. She was probably coming down with the flu. That morning, she had thrown up most of her breakfast, which was a shame because the porridge had turned out really well for a change.

These dreams were getting more and more precise. She knew without a shadow of a doubt that the conversation between Nicky and Sepp she had just heard was about to take place very shortly, within the hour. They were coming closer.

Cat swung her feet off the edge of the box bed and stood up.

Then she fainted.

CHAPTER 14

C AT BECAME CONSCIOUS TO the scent of lavender and the feeling of something cool and moist on her forehead.

"There," said Ouska's matter-of-fact voice close to her head, sounding pleased, "she's coming round; I thought she would."

Cat noticed she was lying on the bed again; she could feel the linen sheet under her and the soft woollen blanket lightly covering her. The mattress moved, and she opened her eyes to see Guy take the place on the edge of the bed that Ouska had just vacated.

"Catriona Karana!" he said, his voice edged with worry, "what happened? You frightened me!" He took her hand and kissed the back of her fingers. Cat blinked, then smiled at him. She loved it when he called her by that special name; he only used it for the ones most precious to him.

"I don't know what happened," she said, surprised at how weak she sounded. "I—I had a nap, I think—a long one—and then I remember trying to get up—and that's all."

He turned his head with a frown, looking at Ouska who was wringing out a cloth in a dish of lavender water. Cat noticed that Andy stood by the workshop door, looking out from under his black eyebrows with concern in his eyes, Bibby clinging to his hand. "What's wrong with Cat?" Guy asked his aunt harshly, "what is it? Is she ill? Is there something you can do? When will she get better?"

"I expect by about late July or early August," said Ouska laconically, draping the cloth over the edge of the bowl. "There is nothing wrong, boy, don't fret yourself."

"August?" said Cat, bewildered. Her head was still swimming. "Why August?"

Guy looked at her with shock on his face. "Nine months," he said.

Cat's eyes grew wide. "You mean I'm *pregnant?!?*" She burst into tears.

Guy's eyebrows drew down in a frown. He pressed his clenched fist to his mouth, glowered at Cat, then at Ouska, jumped up from the bed, turned his back on the women, and marched off past Bibby and Andy into his workshop.

Bibby let go of the boy's hand, pattered across the floor, and clambered up on the bed beside Cat.

"Mumma?" she asked, her big turquoise eyes round. She gently patted Cat's stomach. "Mumma baby!" she announced. "Mumma no cwy!"

"That's right, dear. Mama is having a baby," said Ouska, taking the place on the edge of the bed again. "It'll be well, child, don't fret yourself."

"I'm not!" sobbed Cat. "I don't even know why I'm crying! It's just—just—I don't know! I didn't expec—he c—hect..."

"No cwy, Mumma," said Bibby, patting Cat's cheek, "no fwet!"

Cat gave a watery chuckle through her sobs. Ouska handed her a handkerchief and helped her to sit up, and Cat blew her nose.

"What happened?" she asked, her voice still clogged with tears. "How come you're here?"

"Well, it appears the sound of you falling woke the little one from her nap. She fetched her dad, who did not stay nearly as calm as the babe on finding you on the floor, and he set the boy running through the Wald for me." Cat looked to the corner of the room where Andy had stood, but he was no longer there. He must have followed Guy back into the workshop.

"Did Andy find you?" she asked.

"Yes, he did. For all he will not speak, his look alone would have told me there was need. But he met me halfway down the path; I had already set out—I knew there was something amiss. Oh, not with you, rightly," she patted Cat's hand, "but I knew you would need my help. Your man was in such a fret as I've rarely seen him in. He'll be all right now, I reckon."

Cat smiled through the drying tears on her face. "*He'll* be all right?" she asked. "What about me? I thought I was the one who passed out."

Ouska chuckled. "So you were. You'll be fine, for certain; there is nothing here that feels wrong. All is as it should be." She took Cat's hand in her brown work-worn one, and with her other hand stroked back the hair from Cat's forehead. "You'll do well, child."

Cat drew a wobbly breath. "Will I?" she asked. "I have no idea what—so I passed out from this? And—wait—is that why I was sick early today? Morning sickness?"

"Mumma yick!" Bibby told Ouska importantly. "Mumma go fump! Mumma better now?" she asked Cat and climbed into her lap.

"Yes, Mama is better," Cat told her and wrapped her arms, still a bit shaky, around the little girl. "Thank you for fetching Papa and Andy, that was clever of you." She turned to Ouska. "What do I need to do, Aunt? Am I going to be sick all the time? Am I going to keep passing out? I don't know anything about pregnancy! And are you sure about August?"

"Fairly certain. I can feel it," said Ouska. "Does it fit with your time?"

"Oh—oh yes, I suppose it does. It's been about a month—actually, more like six weeks, I think."

"There you are, then. And as for the illness, there's no telling. You might have a bad time of it; some women do. But it's nothing out of the usual, and it'll pass after a threemonth or so. I'll look out a brew to help; there's more than one herb that will ease it. You do need to take care not to stand up too quick, specially from lying down or bending over, but I see no cause for another swoon. And your man is likely to walk on eggshells around you now," she chuckled, "if he's as much like his father in this as in everything else."

"Ouska—" Cat started, then gave the little girl in her arms a quick squeeze. "Go see Papa for a minute," she told her, and Bibby hopped off the bed and padded along to the workshop. "Aunt," Cat started again, "why did Guy look at me that way? I——I think he's angry."

"Your man's a bit of a fool at times," Ouska said matter-of-factly, "but you'd best ask him yourself. That's a matter between man and wife; I don't try to speak for him. I have a shrewd idea what went through that fool head of his, but as I say, you need to speak with him your own self. I think you had best rest a mite more for now; you're still a bit white around the edges. Be easy on yourself, and it should be well." She suddenly gave Cat a bright smile. "Well, child, I must say I haven't been this pleased in some time. It's a right good thing, your carrying a little one. You'll be a fine mother to it, just like you are to the babe here. It was a good day for this family when you dropped through from Outland, a very good day."

Cat's eyes were filling up with tears again, and she sniffled into the handkerchief. "Thank you, Aunt. That means a lo- ho- hot..." She got the hiccups. "I don't eve—hic—even know why I'm so—hic—weepy to-day—hic. I suppo—hic——ose it's hor—hic—mones or some—hic—thing..."

"I don't know what those might be, but it happens right often that women get weepy when they expect. Nothing wrong with that. Tell your man I said that. Now you go take your rest; I'll let the young fool know you need to sleep. The babe can play in his shop for the time being; don't fret yourself over her."

Cat gratefully sank back against her pillows. She did still feel unusually tired. Ouska drew the blanket over her shoulders, closed the doors of the box bed most of the way, and made her way out of the room. Cat nodded off. A mouse rustled in the corner of the room.

Sepp's voice. "How're you doing, old man? Hey, Ben—look at me. How are you?"

"Fine." Ben's voice quiet, gruff.

"Brought you a tea—Nicky made it. You want it?"

"Whatever."

"Hey—hey hey. Don't grouch at me like that, it's not my fault."

"Sorry."

"All right then, don't worry about it. What are you doing?"

"Just some YouTube."

"Find anything interesting?"

"Not really."

"Hey, what's this?"

"Oh, just this singer. It's that Av—Av—"

Coughing.

"Whoa. Deep breath, boy. Come on, have a sip of the tea. There. Better now? Good. So what was that? Let me see. Af-ril La-fig-nee?"

"Av—Av—..." Coughing. "Laveen."

"Oh, Avril Lavigne. That's how you say that? Hmm. Is she any good?"

Raspy breaths. "Yeah. She's okay, I guess. Kinda old, but not bad. Thanks for the tea, Sepp."

"No problem, old man. Are you sure you're all right?"

"Yeah, yeah. Just want to—you know. Chill."

"Okay. Nicky and I will be in the living room, if you need us."

"Yeah, sure. Whatever."

"Drink your brew, youngling. 'Bye!"

"Huh?"

The sound of a door closing. Steps moving down a hallway.

Sepp's voice. "He started choking again. At the name of some singer woman he found on the computer. There is something very wrong here, Nicky."

"Yes, I know. He did that the other day, too. Except—are you sure it was a woman? I thought it was a guy. Some actor."

"No, this was a woman, very much so. Long blonde hair and all."

"Yeah, okay, not the same thing then. The other time, it was a guy, definitely, short dark hair. An actor, like I said. Brian somebody—he shortens it. Br—whatever. Holden, that's it! Brian Holden. Brolden. Ben was having an absolute choking fit. I wouldn't even have known he was looking up this guy—YouTube, did you say? Maybe that was it. He was on it that time, too. I wouldn't have known anything of it—I don't really care what he's doing online, I think he's pretty trustworthy—I was just trying to make conversation. Asking him what he was looking at. And when he tried to tell me, he started choking."

"Yes, that's exactly what happened just now! April—no, Avril. That was the name. He could say the second part well enough. I can't think of it now."

"Avril Lavigne?"

112

"Yes, that."

"Avril, and Brolden. You're right, this is getting weirder by the day."

"Did you get through to the school on the telephone?"

"Yes, I did. They'll have his records ready for me to pick up in the morning, and I can sign the papers to withdraw him for the time being. I hope this gives us some breathing space... Oh God, I wish I hadn't used just that phrase. Oh Sepp... Does stuff like this happen in your world?"

The sound fading, to be replaced by the faint, far-away signal. Different voices this time, two men.

"The accursed black traitors have found the way to the land to which the slave was sent. You will go. Find our servant, but more important, find the slave. It was not sufficient to remove him from this land; he must be destroyed."

"But, my lord, there is only one more stone—your humble servant may not be able to return to our glorious land, your humble servant may be lost as the other was lost, and no one knows if..."

"Silence! They have sent a man to seek him, to bring him here, and to use him for their accursed ends against our person. You will go, you will find him. The cursed machinations of the black traitors will be brought to an end. Go! Go now, or you shall suffer the consequences!"

"Yes, my lord; please do not be angered with your humble servant, my lord! Your humble servant goes to do your bidding, my lord..."

CHAPTER 15

C AT WOKE UP TO dusk falling outside and the smell of stew cooking in the room. She pushed open the door of the box bed and peered out. Guy was at the hearth, stirring something in the big black cast iron cooking pot, while Bibby was kneeling on a chair by the table, busily chopping a potato into odd-sized chunks with a dull table knife. Guy picked up the cutting board and his razor-sharp chopping knife and carried them over to the table. Cat swung her feet over the edge of the bed, fished for her shoes with her bare toes, and very carefully and slowly stood up. No dizziness—good. She padded over to the table, looking over Guy's shoulder.

"What are you chop—" She broke off as the full impact of the garlic on the cutting board assaulted her nostrils, and a wave of nausea washed over her. Clapping her hand over her mouth, she rushed out through the back door in the workshop, slamming it behind her to keep the cold out of the cottage. But she did not quite make it to the privy before she threw up, thoroughly. Through her retching, she heard the door creak open, close again, then open once more. Guy appeared beside her with a wet cloth and a cup of water.

"Here," he said curtly, holding out the cloth. "I'm sorry."

"Thank you," said Cat weakly, leaning against the wood stack beside the privy to support her shaking legs. "I think it was the garlic; all of a sudden it made me sick." She wiped her face with the cloth, then held out a shaking hand for the cup and took a few sips. "This is a real pain if I'm going to be throwing up like that all the time."

"I'm sorry," he said again, with a frown.

"Well, it's not like there's anything you can do about it—not like it's your fault. Then again, I suppose it is," she said with a smile, starting to feel a little better already.

"I *said* I was sorry!" he snapped, yanked open the privy door, and hauled out the water bucket Cat insisted on keeping there for washing hands. He dumped the water on the puddle of vomit beside the door. It washed away into a little dip, where it slowly seeped into the ground.

"Hey!" said Cat, with a frown of her own, "what's all that about? You didn't know the garlic would make me sick—I didn't even know myself—and I was just kidding about the other—you know..."

He banged the bucket on the ground.

"Were you?" he asked. "It *is* my fault! I know that! And I'm sorry that carrying my child is making you unhappy! I'm sorry that you are ill because of it! I'm sorry, all right?" He snatched the bucket back up by its handle and turned away to head to the water pump around the corner of the shop.

"Wait just a second!" said Cat, catching him by the back of his washleather vest. She hauled him to a stop and pulled him around to face her. "Is that what this is about? You think I'm unhappy about being pregnant?"

His scowl turned to a look of uncertainty. "You cried..."

"Ah!" Cat nodded. "Your aunt specifically said to tell you, my dear man, that (and I quote) 'it happens right often that women get weepy when they expect' (end quote). And she should know, wouldn't you think?"

"Oh—you mean you cried because—well, because..."

"I don't know why I cried, dear. Surprise, I think. In fact, I'm still feeling a bit—" she blinked, "a bit weepy right now, and having my man yell and glower at me doesn't help." She sniffled and wiped the back of her hand over the tip of her nose.

"I'm sorry..." he said again, helplessly.

"Oh you!" said Cat. She reached up, cupped his cheeks in her hands, and turned his face down towards her, forcing him to look into her eyes. "Listen to me, Dyniselm Septimissimus! I am very, *very* happy to be pregnant, and I am proud to be carrying your child! *Our* child. You got that? I'm *happy*. And the only thing that would make me *un*happy about all this is if you were to carry on in this snit of yours and keep apologizing all day long! I can take the sickness, but I can't take your moods, all right? Got it?"

"Do you mean it?" he said slowly, lowering the bucket to the ground. "You mean it!" he suddenly cried triumphantly, caught her up in his arms and swung her around in a circle, whooping with delight. Cat clutched onto him and squealed.

"Control yourself," she laughed breathlessly when he stood her back on her feet, "what kind of example are you going to set for your son if you can't keep your emotions in check?"

"Son?" he said, his eyebrows rising right up to his hairline, "did you say 'son'?"

Cat tipped her head sideways, as if she was listening. "Yes, I did, didn't I?" she said. "I only just realized!" She laid a hand on her still-flat stomach. "Son. It's a boy, this one here, I know it. Oh Guy!" she cried, suddenly deliriously happy, "we're having a baby!" She flung herself into his arms and hugged him as hard as she could. He didn't seem to mind.

All of a sudden Cat noticed the soft, cold wetness that had been settling on them for some minutes now. "It's snowing," she said. "How long has this been going on?"

"Not very long, I think," Guy said, and peered through the dusk at the thickening snowfall. "But it's coming down fast. Get yourself in the house, Madam Wife, you're expecting, you can't stand about in the cold!"

"Yes, sir, right away, sir," said Cat, holding up her skirts and bobbing a curtsy while sticking out her tongue at him. He wrinkled his nose at her, took up the bucket again, and disappeared around the back of the shop to refill it.

Cat came back into the cottage and stopped dead at the sight that met her eyes. Bibby knelt at the table, the cutting board with a long carrot in front of her, wielding the razor-sharp butcher knife. *Chop*—a chunk flew off the end of the carrot—*chop*!

Cat sucked in a lungful of air, then forced herself to speak calmly. "Sweetie? That's a really sharp knife! Can you give it to Mama please?"

"Bibby helping!" the little girl said proudly. "Andy and Bibby helping!"

Cat only now noticed the boy, directly at Bibby's elbow. His hand hovered over the little girl's arm, ready to grasp her hand if she made one false move. Cat gave him a speaking glance and blew out her breath in relief. He ducked his head and gave a slight shrug with one shoulder.

"Bibby wanna helping!" said Bibby again, "Andy helping Bibby helping!"

Cat looked around the debris on the table, and understanding dawned. She well knew her little stepdaughter's stubbornness; if Bibby took it into her head to use the sharp knife, it would take some doing to stop her. She'd probably grabbed it before Andy knew what was happening, and it looked like the boy, instead of fighting her for the knife, had instead given her the safest vegetable she could cut with it——an extra-long carrot that kept the little hand holding it far away from the sharp blade—and had guided her hands to keep her from hurting herself.

Cat shook her head. It looked like Guy had rushed out after her without even putting the knife out of reach. It was very unlike him to forget his daughter's safety even for one second; he must have been desperately worried about her. Thank goodness Andy had been there. The boy was showing some unsuspected sides.

"Mama needs the knife now, sweetie," Cat told the little girl, "you can take the other one, okay?" She gave Bibby back the table knife and convinced her to let go of the sharp chopping knife. "See, you didn't finish cutting the potato, you do that." Bibby let herself be persuaded. Andy wordlessly took the mostly empty water bucket from beside the front door, and went outside with it.

Guy came back in with him, their heads and shoulders completely covered in white.

"It's coming down hard," said Guy, "we'd better get in a few loads of wood for the fire."

"Can you finish putting together the stew please? I don't know if I can stand smelling it while it's cooking, I think I'd better stay away from the hearth," said Cat.

"Oh, all right. Andy, could you..." But the boy was already gone from the room. "Where is he?"

"He went out back as soon as you said we needed wood. Guy, he just"—she lowered her voice with a glance at the little girl—"he just saved Bibby from chopping her fingers off—you forgot the knife on the table, and she took it into her head that she needed to use it. Andy kept right beside her. Who knows what would have happened without him there!"

Guy went pale. "I did what? Oh dear. Yes, the boy is becoming very helpful—although..."

There was a thump at the workshop door, and Andy came through with an armful of firewood. He dumped it in the holder by the stove and went right back outside.

"Although what?" asked Cat.

"I'll tell you later; I have to get this food ready, and I might as well give the boy a hand with the wood."

CHAPTER 16

B Y THE TIME THEY were finished with supper, the snow was already three inches deep, and the wind was picking up. Cat could hear the snowflakes hissing as they hit the inside of the chimney pipe.

"Ooh, cozy," she said with a comfortable little shiver. "Nothing like a good warm fire on a cold evening! Is there going to be lots of snow, do you think?"

"Probably," Guy said. "It's usual this time of year. Only four more weeks to solstice. There've been years where I barely made it through the snow to get to the solstice feast."

"Oh, yeah, the feast! Is that like the equinox feast that we had in town in September?"

Guy laughed. "No, not quite—it's about ten times as big. The hall is usually filled to overflowing. The solstice feasts are the biggest ones of the year; all of Ruph and the surrounding areas come decked out in finery. Which reminds me, I need to look out my feast clothing; the mice had better not have got into it."

"Feast clothing? You mean everyone dresses up? But," Cat's eyes were wide, "I don't have anything to wear!" Then she laughed. "Listen to me! *I don't have anything to wear*," she repeated in a high-pitched, affected voice, wringing her hands theatrically and fluttering her eyelashes. "*Oh dearie me, whatever shall I do?*"

Guy grinned. "I'm sure we can find something," he said. "And Andy here can probably wear one of my older vests; mine is new just from two years ago, and I'm sure I saved the old one."

"Where?" asked Cat. "I don't remember seeing any clothing other than what's in the trunk—are there hidey-holes in this house I *still* haven't found?"

"Looks that way. It's under the trunk; there's a cedar-lined space for the special things. We need to get at them anyway, it's getting cold and we need the featherbeds."

"Oh, wow—we've got featherbeds? Why didn't I know about that?"

"Well," Guy grinned at her, "I didn't want you getting too warm in bed; when you're cold, you cuddle up..."

"Shush!" Cat swatted him, giving a self-conscious glance at the kids. He laughed.

"So, Sir Husband," Cat stood up from the table and looked down at him, arms akimbo, "featherbeds?"

"Feavverbed, feavverbed," sang Bibby through a mouthful of apple she was munching for dessert. Andy looked at her sideways from under his eyebrows and gave a slight twitch to the corner of his mouth. Almost a smile, but not quite.

Guy got the boy to help him move aside the clothing chest that stood in the corner of the room beside the box bed. It was their closet and chest of drawers all at once. They didn't have a lot of clothes between the lot of them—two or three outfits each was all they needed. Cat loved the simplicity of it all, but she admitted to herself that it could sometimes get a little monotonous to always wear the same skirt, blouse, and simple moccasins, day in and day out. Something a little special would be welcome.

Sure enough, underneath the trunk was yet another trapdoor. Cat wondered if this was the last one in the house she hadn't seen yet, or if, in fact, the whole house had these hidden cupboards under it.

Guy pulled up the trapdoor, which, like all the others in the house, was a section of floor planks with a knot hole to lift it up by. It took him some effort to get the flap to rise, and when it finally opened, Cat saw why. Unlike the other storage holes in the house, this was not just a compartment under the floor but was lined with a fine-grained, closely jointed darker wood. In fact, Cat realized, it was a snug-lidded cedar trunk built directly into the floor.

"That's neat," she said, "so then the mice probably didn't get in, did they?"

"I most devoutly hope not!" said Guy, reaching into the hole and pulling out a thick, pouffy duvet covered in a quilted patchwork of browns and greens. He tossed it at Cat, who caught it in both arms.

"Mmm," she said, "it smells so nice and cedary!" She shook out the quilt and spread it over their bed. Guy was still rooting around in the storage space.

"I cannot find my feast clothing!" he muttered, sounding annoyed. "Ah, there's Bibby's—oh."

"What?"

"It's Bibby's from last year," he said, shaking out a little gown made of a soft, gold-brown fabric. "It's much too small now! I didn't think. Well, I suppose she'll need a new one, too."

"Bibby dwess?" asked the little girl, reaching for the outfit.

"No, sweetie, it's too little for you now—you're such a big girl, it won't fit any more!" Cat said.

"Bibby dwess!" she insisted, and Guy gave it to her. She wanted to try it on right away, and Cat felt too tired to argue. It was a lovely little gown; the year before, when Bibby was only a year old and had just started to walk, it would have reached right down to her ankles. The sides were laced up with golden yellow cords, with matching embroidery around the neckline. Bibby wiggled out of her tunic. "Put on dwess!" she demanded, and Cat tried to pull the little gown over her head. Bibby got stuck.

"I'm sorry, sweetie, it just won't fit!" said Cat, hoping against hope that they weren't in for another tantrum.

"Bibby dwess!" came the muffled complaint through the folds of the gown. Cat tugged it off again, and saw that Bibby's chin was wobbling.

"Oh, come on, sweetie..."

"Bibby, look!" called Guy, theatrically, "look what I found!" With the air of a conjurer, he pulled out of the storage a dark green garment, a man's vest similar in pattern to the leather one he had been wearing ever since the days had got cooler.

"Is that yours?" asked Cat curiously. "So you found it?"

"No, this is my old one, not the one I was looking for." He gasped dramatically as if he had suddenly thought of something. "Bibby, do you think Andy can wear this?"

His ploy worked.

"Andy dwess?" Bibby asked, her eyes round. Cat thought she saw Andy break into an almost-smile.

"Andy's vest, yes," she said, taking the vest from Guy and holding it out to the boy. He looked at her with wide eyes, and made no move to take it.

"Here, try it on!" said Cat, pushing the vest towards him. He pulled back just a bit.

"Come on, boy," said Guy, "I don't wear it any more; you might as well have it! If you have nothing to wear for the feast, we can't very well take you along, and Mistress Cat will feel bad because you're sitting home alone and won't enjoy herself. Then she'll take it out on me—you know how she gets when she's unhappy."

Cat swatted him.

"See?" Guy said. "You'd better take it!"

Cat smacked him again.

"No hit, Mumma!" Bibby scolded, and made everyone laugh. Andy lost his frightened look.

"Papa was being cheeky," Cat said to Bibby, "but I won't hit him again if he promises to be good, and if Andy tries on the vest."

Bibby grabbed the vest out of Cat's hands and shoved it at the boy. "Andy twy on dwess!"

He gave his little almost-smile and slipped the vest on over his plain brown tunic. The turquoise embroidery along the neckline and down the front of the vest was set off against the dark green cloth, a felt-like material with a beautiful drape to it. Wool, perhaps? The pale blue of the decorative stitching emphasized the olive tone of Andy's skin and drew attention to his dark eyes. The vest fit well enough; it was just a little too wide across the back.

"I guess you're a bit broader in the shoulders," Cat said to Guy. "Can we get this altered to fit him properly? I don't think my sewing skills are up to doing it myself."

"Certainly, we can take it to Torgha Taylor's to be made to fit. Oh! That's what happened to my new one! I got a little tear in it last solstice feast, and I had taken it to Torgha's to be mended. I think Aunt picked it up for me, and it must still be at her house. The rest of my clothes, too; we stayed the night after the feast there."

A sudden wind blast rattled the outside of the cottage, and howled around the corners.

"Whoa!" said Cat, "that was a big one! I've never actually heard wind whistling around a house before—I only read about it—but this one sure does whistle. What's it looking like out there?" She went to peer out through the window. "I can't even see anything out there, it's blowing so much!" She stepped over to the cottage door, unlatched the hook, and pulled open the door a few inches. "Oy!" she called out, having to suddenly lean hard against the door as snow blew in through the crack. "That's a humdinger of a storm, and it wants to come in!" The snow was whirling hard past the door; Cat could barely make out the trees on the other side of the clearing. Then Guy was behind her, helping her push the door shut and latching it again. Cat brushed at the snow on the floor with her foot. "Is that an extra-bad storm, or is this normal?"

"Neither," said Guy laconically. "It's a fairly strong one, but I've seen worse. Why, don't they have snowstorms in your old world?"

"Well, not where I come from. When it snows, it's usually just some slush, and it doesn't last long. We mostly get rain in the winter. But there are areas in my country where this would probably be considered a gentle and mild snowfall—it's just that I've never lived in any of those places."

They turned around to the kids. Andy looked slightly stunned and was rubbing his hands on his arms, shivering.

"Hey, what is it, boy?" said Guy. "Haven't you ever seen a snowstorm before? Here," he knelt by the storage hole again, and fished around in the bottom, "you'll want this." He pulled out another thick fluffy quilt, this one patterned in green and blue squares, and dumped it into Andy's arms, not giving him a chance to refuse this time. "Take it to your bed; that should keep you warm tonight. It's not that cold here though, is it?" he asked Cat.

"Not in here, I think—but then, I'm used to colder temperatures, just not this amount of snow. But I think," she said, looking questioningly at the boy, "Andy might be from a much warmer climate—aren't you?"

Andy was hugging the quilt to himself and gave that tiny shrug of his shoulder that Cat was starting to interpret as the equivalent of "I guess so".

"Well, you'd better keep warm, then," said Cat briskly. "Stay close to the fire, wrap up warm, and you'll get used to it eventually. Most people do. You just have to know how to cope, how to protect yourself from it. Actually, hot drinks help quite a lot, too. Anyone for some mintbrew?" She fetched the kettle from the shelf by the fire and shook it to see if there was any water left. "Hmm, empty. Would you... No, never mind. We'll take the water from the bucket."

"Bibby mintboo!" said the little girl. "Mintboo and more appa!"

"More apple? Oh—sure, why not. You can share another apple with Andy, if he wants." Cat smiled at the boy, who wore the quilt wrapped around his shoulders by now and had stopped shivering. He held the quilt with one hand and with the other collected an apple from the storage bucket under the shelf.

Cat and Guy were snugly closed into their box bed, the snowstorm still howling fiercely outside, when he picked up the thread of their earlier conversation.

"Andy's a good lad, he is," he said to Cat, who was cuddled into the hollow of his shoulder, "and he learns quickly. But there's something odd going on. I haven't taught him on the wheel yet; he needs to learn to wedge and hand-form first, but he does well enough at what I taught him so far. He has an affinity for the clay; there is something right about what he does. I give him a lump of clay, and he does the wedging to get it ready for me to throw. I swear he's learned to work the clay properly; when I watch him wedging, he does it right, and fast enough, too. But there have been a few times where the pieces he prepared for me were unusable, every last one of them. Every single piece I try to throw either has air pockets in it, or the clay is so uneven that even coning it up won't get it straight."

Cat was used to her husband's potter's talk and had been mentally translating as he spoke.

"There is something not right about the way he kneads the clay, so you can't make things from it on the wheel?"

"Well, not always; that's the issue! After the first time that happened, I watched him do the wedging—I was ready to correct him, see where he went wrong so he could learn it right—but he did everything just as I had taught him, and that day everything went smoothly. You know that set of straight-sided cups with the twist-ed handles, two dozen of them—that was his wedging work. There was no problem. But the next day, I could not make one single piece from the clay he had pre-pared. Air bubbles, off-kilter pieces that I could barely centre—you tell me what that could be! It's as if he had hardly wedged it at all, just slapped it together quickly to make it look as if he had, not properly worked it hard like it's meant to be."

Cat wiggled her head deeper against his chest and wrapped her arm around his waist.

"But this never happens when you've watched him do it?" she asked.

"No, that's the odd thing. I don't know *what* he is doing..."

"Were you even in the room when he was wedging the bad pieces?"

He was silent for a minute. "No," he said slowly, "no, now that you mention it—I was not. The first time was after I had gone to fetch more clay from the clay hole. And one time I was outside, getting the kiln ready for firing, and another time in town doing a delivery. Each time he had most of the wedged pieces ready when I came back; I thought nothing of it because he had had enough time to do them while I was gone. Do you think—what *do* you think?"

"I don't know either, but obviously he's doing something differently when you're not watching. I guess you just need to keep your eyes peeled. Mmm, you're so nice and toasty..."

CHAPTER 17

T HE NEXT MORNING, CAT was kneading the dough for that day's bread—it came more easily every time now—and she was listening through the door to the workshop, which stood a little ajar, to Guy talking to Andy. There was not a sound to be heard from the boy; he simply never spoke, or laughed, or made any other noise. He even moved quietly—except for when he was thumping clay around with his master.

"You have to work with what the clay wants," Guy said. "The potter's hands know what the clay is meant to be. Well," (Cat could tell from the tone of his voice that he was scratching his head at that moment, probably smearing himself with clay) "well, mine do, anyway. I think most real clay workers are like that. My brother, he works in wood; his hands tell him what the wood wants to be. I don't know wood—one piece is like the next to me——and he doesn't know clay, but looking at each other's work, we can see it's right. And the wood, and the clay—or the stone or metal or what-have-you—each piece can be different. One piece can come from the same lump of clay as another, but one is a cup, and another a bowl." Cat heard the rhythmic thumping of Guy smacking the clay on the table to work air bubbles out of the piece, offset by the slower, but no less vigorous, thumps of Andy imitating his teacher. "No two workers work the same," Guy continued. "A real workman can make the stuff do what he wants, of course, to a point. But it's misusing the craft to force the material into a form it's not meant to be." A final thump, and Cat could hear Guy's steps as he went to fetch another tool——a damp cloth, judging by his next words. "Let's cover this lot up; we need to get to work clearing the snow from the yard." Cat heard the scraping of the stool as it was pushed under the work table.

Guy's head appeared around the door frame to the workshop. Cat bit back a smile—as expected, he had a big streak of red-brown clay up his left temple going right into his hair.

"The boy and I are going to start clearing a path through the snow; it's a good ell deep out there, deeper in places. When we're done, do you want to try to make it through to town? Or do you want me to go fetch you something from Aunt, or from the shops?"

"Well—I don't know if I feel like traipsing through knee-deep snow right now. I might if I had some mukluks and ski pants, but with these skirts..."

"Muk-whats and what kind of pants?" Guy asked, raising his eyebrows.

"Mukluks—they're a kind of tall fur boot for walking in the snow. Like those," she pointed at the calf-high pair of moccasins slouched beside the front door, "except with fur on the outside, or inside, or both. And ski pants, I suppose you would call them trousers. Skiing is gliding around on sticks, or planks. It's usually done down hills, but sometimes on the flat, too."

"Oh, snow gliders! Yes, of course. And, well, yes, I suppose wearing trousers would be more practical for that, less draughty. In fact, I remember Yldra using her brothers' legwear for doing it when we were kids. Charn and Chonyk didn't mind having a pair of their old trousers stolen, but they did care when she out-raced them on the gliders. That was quite a long time ago though."

"Ah yes, ages and ages, you're such an old man now ..." Cat took a damp cloth and wiped the clay off the side of Guy's face. "Do you have skis—snow gliders?"

Guy caught her hand, took the cloth away, and pressed a quick kiss into her palm. "Yes, there is a pair out in the woodshed, but the snow is hardly deep enough for it yet. So, if you don't want to come to town then, do you have any commission for your devoted servant?" He rubbed at his temple with the cloth.

"Here, let me finish, you're just making it worse," Cat said, reclaiming the washcloth. "You might ask Aunt if she has any dried parsley or savoury to spare. The soup just isn't as good without it."

"I could do that—but what about the herbs in the garden? There are clumps of both of those in the herb bed by the house."

"Well, yes, but they'll be frozen to mush now, won't they?"

"Not necessarily. The snow does not freeze things right away, in fact, it protects them. And those two are quite tough; they do not get blighted by the smallest frost like some of the other herbs. I'll clear a path into the garden, shall I, and you can go see for yourself, even in your flimsy women's clothing." He smiled at her as he slipped his feet into his moccasin boots, then pulled his dark brown cloak off the hook behind the door, and took down Cat's lighter brown one for Andy to use. "That boy needs some warmer clothing, too; he's still shivering at the slightest draught. I was going to take him with me to town, but he might be better off staying here in the warm. Say," a thought struck him, "if he's never seen snow before, he won't have any idea how to go about clearing it!"

An hour later, Guy and Andy came stomping back into the house, their noses, cheeks, and hands bright red from the cold. Andy was not shivering, which Cat took for a good sign; shovelling snow was warm business. She would have to hurry with those mittens she was knitting for Guy and then start a pair for Andy; they would make good gifts for the solstice feast. She poured them both a cup of mintbrew she had kept hot on the stove.

"It's just as I thought," Guy said, "there is lots of parsley and savoury left under the snow, and sage, thyme, and some lavender still, as well. I think you picked all the basil and the more tender herbs, did you not?"

"Yes, Aunt told me to, and the mint, too. There is the last of it." She gestured up at the bundles of herbs hanging off some drying lines strung across the corner of the cottage. "I'm glad she did. There's just so much I don't know yet about gardening, and cooking, and keeping house..."

Guy gently flicked her nose with his forefinger. "You're doing very well, Madam Wife. I left the herbs in the garden for you to pick; I don't know how much you want in the soup. There's a good path cleared to get to it. Andy, when you are finished with your brew there is some work to do in the shop; that should keep you warm if the shovelling hasn't warmed you enough yet. First lesson of winter: keep moving and the cold won't get to you." He smiled his lopsided smile at his apprentice.

Andy looked at him over the edge of his cup and gave his minute shoulder shrug. Cat felt that there was an affinity developing between the two of them, and she was glad.

Guy left for town, and Andy took himself into the workshop, closing the door behind him.

Two hours later, the bread was nearly done baking, and Cat's soup gently bubbled away on the stove top. It was a lovely thick soup with brown beans, dried tomatoes, chunks of onions, and some crumbled hot peppers; now she needed the herbs. She swung her cloak around her shoulders, took along the kitchen knife, and stepped outside, pulling the door shut behind her. Following the nice little path the men had dug around the side of the house, she found the spot where Guy had cleared the snow away from the herbs. Sure enough, there was lots of parsley, looking not much the worse for wear, and the savoury shrub just beside it. She cut several sprigs from both plants, found some chives on the other side of the parsley as well, and made her way back to the house.

The front door wouldn't open.

What happened? *Oh*, thought Cat, *the latch must have fallen and got stuck; it's locked the door like it did that time before.* Except last time Guy had opened the door from the inside. This time, Bibby was napping, and Andy—oh, of course, Andy was in the workshop. She could just go in that way.

Cat made her way around the side of the house, her feet crunching on the gravel under the snow. As she passed the workshop window, she heard a curious noise from inside. *Whap whap whap whap whap!* It sounded as if something was being hit with a giant fly swatter. The workshop door was in need of grease, it squeaked rather loudly. When Cat stepped into the workshop, there was Andy, wedging the last of the lumps of clay that Guy had set him to do, turning it into the round ram's head shape that was necessary for throwing pots on the wheel. A number of other lumps sat on the table under a damp cloth.

"Hey, almost finished?" Cat asked in a friendly tone. "I hope Master Guy comes back soon; the soup and the bread are nearly done. Are you hungry?"

But the boy would not look at her, and his face was a deep red. *He looks—guilty!* thought Cat. *What's been going on here?* She shrugged and carried her herbs into the kitchen.

———ell———

"Again!" Guy said, more than a little irritated, that evening to Cat in the privacy of their bed. "One whole set of wedged clay pieces useless. What *has* that boy been doing? There is something not right here! Not only is the clay not properly wedged—it's like I am putting it to the wrong purpose. I can no longer feel what it wants done with it after the boy has been at it, doing whatever he is doing when he's alone."

"I can feel something," said Cat slowly. "There is something there. I feel a danger, mostly to Andy, but there's more to it than just him. It's something unsavoury, trying to destroy, trying to—to gnaw its way through, trying to take what doesn't belong to it. It feels revolting, like vermin—but it has Andy in its grip somehow." She sighed. "I wish he would speak. Do you think he cannot, or will not? He understands well enough——in fact, I believe he has quite sharp hearing. You know, I think he heard me coming around the house earlier, and thought it was you—and he did something weird in there." She told him about the strange noise and the even stranger reaction from Andy at her stepping into the shop.

Guy frowned. "I cannot think what he might have been doing," he said, "but I'm going to get behind this. The first thing I need to do is to oil those door hinges."

"Sounds like a plan," said Cat drowsily, and gave a big yawn. "Good grief, I'm sleepy all of a sudden..." She snuggled against Guy's side, closed her eyes, and was almost instantly asleep.

CHAPTER 18

*T*HE SOUND OF A TV *running in the background. Steps entering the room, then Nicky's voice, upset. "Man, that was freaky! That rat guy almost caught up with us today, with Ben and me——Sepp, I think this guy is stalking us!"*

The TV clicking off. Sepp's voice. "What happened?"

"We were out at the second-hand store, trying to get Ben some new pants—he's growing like a weed, that kid. And then out of the blue he starts that asthma thing again, like he is choking, and there is the rat guy in the next aisle. He didn't see us, though; he was busy pawing through some coats. I got Ben out of there as quickly as I could, and once we were away from that guy and out in the fresh air he got better."

"So now it's just being in the vicinity of this fellow that sets him off?"

"It looks that way. It wasn't at first—when we first met rat guy, Ben was just scared stiff and wouldn't talk, but he could breathe okay. Now he can't even breathe around this creep any more. I don't know what to do, Sepp. We can't call the cops——even if I could, which I can't—"

"Because of Charlie?"

"Yeah, that. I can't call the cops. And even if I did, what would I tell them? 'My nephew gets asthmatic whenever he sees this guy who claims to have known his mom'? I don't think so. What would they do, arrest rat man for living? He hasn't <u>done</u> anything, other than being creepy, you know?"

"Yes, I see. I suppose just knowing that something isn't right makes no impression on the authorities here?"

Nicky's snort. "Not bloody likely. Does it where you're from?"

"Depends who is doing the knowing. If it was my aunt, then yes."

"Must be nice! No, that doesn't work here. They'd want hard evidence, which we haven't got. Sepp, what <u>are</u> we going to do? I have a good mind to go underground, the three of us."

"Underground? You mean move to some kind of cave?"

"Oh, no, not literally; it's just a figure of speech. It means disappear, vanish from circulation, make yourself hard to find. We had to do that a few times when I was a kid when things got too hot for my dad—just packed up a few necessities and disappeared for a while. Moved to a different town, or even farther; once we went clear across the country. I think I'm going to start working on that, get ready to get out of here. That Tyrone guy, he's got me freaked out enough that I think it might be our best option. And it's not like either one of us really has anything keeping us here—now that Cat is gone, the only thing holding me is my job, and I wouldn't be sorry to leave that."

"Could you tell your employer you might leave, ahead of time?"

"I don't think I would dare. It might give the show away. If you're going to do a vanishing act, you don't tell anyone, you just git. Although I suppose it'd be the polite thing to do to at least leave a message for them so they know they can give my job to someone else—Sue Black's been itching for that position for the last couple of years. I guess I could write a note, handing in my resignation, and then mail it on our way out of town. Oh Sepp—this is crazy. I thought I was done with this sort of stuff in my life. But I suppose being Charlie's sister means I'm never done with this kind of crap."

Sepp's voice, serious. "You know, Nicky, I don't believe it's your brother that is the issue here. There's something about Ben—Ben, and that rat fellow. I've been telling you, I've met his kind before."

"Yeah, in your world, I know."

"Yes, in my world. Nicky—you said that because Cat is gone, there is nothing holding you here. Cat is there; she is in Ruph."

"Yeah—but so might be more creepy rat guys!"

"So they might, but we could also have means of dealing with them there, you know. I told you, remember, that my father got rid of that other strange one, when I was a boy..."

Nicky's voice, skeptical. "I thought your dad was gone, Sepp."

"Yes, he is. But my brother is likely more powerful than Father ever was. Nicky, think about it—what better place to vanish to than another <u>world</u>? None of Charlie's old friends—or enemies—could ever get to you again. And the *rat fellow, as I said, we might have ways of dealing with him there."*

"I don't know, Sepp, I don't know if I could handle that... and anyway, how would we get there? Wait a minute——this isn't about your bowl, is it?"

"It is, dear. That is exactly what it is about. I told you; it's the bowl that brought me here. It won't work for me any more, one person can only go one way with it; but I think it might work for you—for you or Ben. I don't know if you can take someone else with you, if they touch you..."

"Whoa, wait a second! What do you mean, it might work for me? What am I supposed to do with it?"

"You just touch it, or look into it. And, well, you disappear from one place and reappear in another."

Nicky's voice, scoffing. "Just like that? Yeah, right! Why hasn't it done it already? I've touched that thing lots of times since you brought it! C'mon—see?"

A loud gasp from Sepp.

"Nicky! Nicky, please don't. Don't do that, don't touch it any more. Not now."

Nicky's voice, a little contrite. "Okay, darlin'. I didn't mean to freak you out; I'm sorry. But it's really not doing anything, is it? The bowl, I mean. You saw."

Sepp's voice, carefully calm. "No, it didn't—this time. But it might have. See, the bowls only take you if you really want to leave. Well, they did—this one is the last one. It's a bit complicated. Once they've taken two people, one way each, they change colour and no longer work. There were six, and five of them are used up. Three of them broke, one brought me here the first time and took Cat back to Ruph, one brought

140

Ashya—Ashley—and took me back, that day at Ryan and Ashley's place, and then there's this one—it brought me here this time, and I think it can take you back. It hasn't, so far, because you had no desire to go away, but now you do. I don't know if it can take more than one person at a time, though, if they touch each other as well as touching the bowl. We would have to risk it."

Nicky's voice rising. "I'm not risking being zapped to some other dimension if I don't even know you'd be coming along! And what about Ben? He's the one who's most at risk here, if you're right! Rat guy is after him, not us! We couldn't just leave him here! If anything, he'd have to be the one to be zapped to your other world! And I can't let him go alone! It wouldn't be right! I'm his guardian——I have to look after him! I don't know what you're thinking, I..."

Sepp's voice, soothing. "Nicky dear. Nicky. Come on, come here. There, don't be hysterical."

Nicky's voice slightly muffled. "I'm not hysterical! Don't think that hugging me is going to make this bet ter... Well, okay, maybe it is. Oh Sepp..."

"It's all right, dear. Promise me, Nicky, that you'll think about this. I believe it is our best chance—Ben's best chance. And you are right—he is the one most at risk. When the time comes, we can try having him be the one to touch the bowl; if we both hold onto him, it might take us along. But if not, he will be taken to Ruph—the other bowls did that, they brought the person to the Arbour, in the Wald—the forest—not far from Guy's house. It happened to Cat, and to me when I went back. If Ben went to them, and we were

141

left here, he would at least be in a safe place; my brother and your friend would look after him."

"Yeah, Cat would, I know that. If you're sure she's there..."

Sepp, seriously. "Yes, Nicky, she is. Believe me."

Nicky's voice, thoughtful. "You know, it's all so weird, but somehow I'm starting to believe you? I still can't totally swallow all this stuff about your other world, and about Cat being there, and magical bowls and whatever. But, well, I trust you... even though you're not making a heck of a lot of sense, but you're just so—so you..." The sound of a kiss, then Nicky's voice, brisk. "Okay, darlin', I'll think about this bowl thing, for you. But I'm still going to make plans for us to disappear the old-fashioned way. I'm going to write that resignation letter for my boss, get it ready for when we need it. And get cash out of the bank, and pack some bags and make sure we have gas in the car. Can you live with that?"

"Yes, as long as you will consider the other way. And promise me to not touch the bowl now, while you make these plans. Please."

"Okay, fine, if it'll make you happy. But what happens if I touch it accidentally?"

"Even that could do it—it's what happened to Cat. But wait, I can touch the bowl; I'll wrap it up. Here, the tablecloth should work." Steps across the room, then Sepp's voice, stern. "There. Don't you dare unwrap that bundle, Miss! Or we would all be very, very sorry."

"Whatever... Hey, don't knock my owl off the mantel. It's my favourite thing ever, next to my new bling. Okay, I'm off to write that letter. No time like the present."

142

CHAPTER 19

I T KEPT SNOWING, OFF and on, for three days. It was on the fourth day that Guy said casually, while spooning up thick breakfast porridge: "I do believe I need to go out for a while today. Is there anything you need me to get in town?"

"No, thank you, dear, we have everything we need. I think I will try to go in on Friday for market day, if the path is clear enough." Cat wiped Bibby's fingers and mouth and untied the little apron the girl was wearing to keep her clothes clean during mealtimes.

"It probably will be; the snow is usually not as deep beneath the trees," said Guy, still in his overly casual tone of voice. Cat realized he was plotting something. Not the best of actors, her husband.

He set out for town shortly after breakfast, wrapped in his cloak and wearing his moccasin boots. Cat got on with household business, wondering how all this was going to work once the baby came. She supposed there would be diapers to deal with. Did one need baby furniture in Ruph? Changing tables or cradles or anything like that? There was hardly any room in the cottage, definitely not now, with the box bed taking up a good chunk of the space. She wondered if eventually they could perhaps extend the cottage, or build upwards, add another story on top. She had been teasing when she suggested it to Guy, but now the idea seemed more and more attractive. There would likely be more babies after this one, and while the cottage was comfortably snug at this point, any more people or furniture would make it crowded to the point of claustrophobia.

Cat went out back to get the laundry off the line, which was strung under the eaves in the lean-to woodshed. It was still damp from the snow blowing onto it, but only a little—she could hang it on the inside rack, which was suspended from the ceiling corner above the clothing trunk, and it should be dry enough by afternoon to be folded and put away. They usually had a fairly wrinkled look to them, all of them. Cat was glad that the people of Ruph did not seem to think that ironing clothes was a necessity; they wore their linen outfits the way they came from the line, clothes peg marks and everything. Cat was comfortable enough with a few wrinkles in her blouse, especially if the alternative was using a flatiron heated on the fire. Ouska had one, or rather, a pair of them; Cat had seen them in her house. But even in town, Ruphians did not seem to be much addicted to finery on an everyday basis; she had never seen Ouska actually *use* the irons.

She brought the armful of damp clothes back in through the workshop. Andy was not in the shop; she stepped over to the window and looked out. Ah, there he was—stacking wood by the kiln. The drying shelves in the shop were quite full; they were getting ready for a firing, during which the kiln needed to be fed around the clock with fuel, so a large quantity of chopped firewood was essential. The boy was working hard, he already had half the stack finished.

Cat took her laundry into the cottage, leaving the workshop door ajar just a little. She got busy hanging the clothes inside and then started on another batch of bread for the next few days.

Halfway through, she heard Andy in the workshop, slamming clay on the board. She stuck her head in the door and looked. He had a large lump out on the table and was slicing it in half and slamming it back together with the rhythmic whacks she was used to hearing from Guy when he worked the clay to remove air pockets. She smiled at the boy, then went back to her own work. It got quiet in the workshop; he was probably wedging the clay pieces now.

Cat took out her knitting and settled in the carved rocking chair which Sepp had made; to date, it was still the most comfortable piece of furniture Cat had ever sat in. Guy's mittens were finished, and she was already most of the way done with the first one for Andy. She wanted to make a pair for Bibby, too, as well as a toque, but the boy needed them sooner than the little girl, who did not, after all, ever have to work outside in the snow.

Bibby was asleep, napping on the big bed. Cat did not like to pull out her trundle bed during the day; it took up too much floor space. Besides, it pulled out from underneath the box bed on the side where the damp laundry was hanging; she did not want Bibby, and the bedding, being dripped on by a piece of wet washing.

Her thoughts strayed to her old world, to Sepp, and to Nicky. And then to the stories she had been reading lately. In the process of sorting the library books into their own version of Dewey Decimal order, Nikor kept finding more tales of Chaelia for her; the shelf by the fireplace was now permanently filled with at least six volumes that she was working her way through. The Rats of Chaelia—it was a curious tale, an epic cycle, almost, of story after story about how the battle raged between those of the Grey Rat, and the Black, back and forth. It was strange that they called themselves the Rats—they definitely were human, not rodents. But their whole society seemed odd, quite archaic, to Cat's mind, even compared to Ruph (never mind the modern world she had left behind), and it was strictly structured into classes and races. They also seemed to rely quite heavily on prophecies and portents and mysterious magic, especially powerful objects. It was all very exotic and quite intriguing. Cat wondered how much of it was truth, and how much fiction. Nikor certainly seemed to think it was real; he refused to shelve the books under 'Mythology'.

Cat grew sleepy, and laid her head against the back of the rocking chair. Her eyes drifted shut, and she dozed off.

Suddenly she was jerked awake by a tremendous noise from the workshop next door.

Whap, whap, whap, wha—and then Guy shouting, yelling at the top of his voice.

"How DARE you! Do not, DO NOT EVER do this again! Do you understand me?!? This is wrong, WRONG! No apprentice of mine will misuse the clay like this!"

Cat sprang up, stumbled over to the workshop, pushed open the door, and nearly tripped down the step that led from the cottage to the workroom. Guy, towering over Andy, was holding the boy's left wrist in an iron grip, and glared at him with fury spewing from his turquoise eyes. The boy cowered away from him. On the table in front of him were several flattened clay pancakes, one half flat and half a small figure, and one complete little figurine, which was sitting at the end of the row. In the middle of the table were what appeared to be several lumps of clay, covered by a damp cloth.

"Guy," Cat said, "Guy! What is it?"

Guy raised his head, glaring at her with deep anger in his eyes. She had not seen him in such a temper since—probably since the day he caught her handling the turquoise bowls. Except then there had been a large amount of fear mixed into his reaction, whereas now he was simply, plainly, furious. She looked steadily into his eyes, trying to draw off some of the anger. "What is it?" she repeated.

He let go of the boy's arm. Andy made a motion with his hand, and Guy snatched at his wrist again.

"No, you will NOT!" he growled at the boy, then reached across him and very carefully picked up the small sculpted figurine from the table. Andy flinched as if he was struck. Guy held the sculpture out of the boy's reach, then let go of his hand.

"THIS is what it is!" he said to Cat, holding out the figurine. Andy suddenly ducked under Guy's arm, spun around on the stool, and bolted out the workshop door. Guy paid him no heed. "This!" he repeated, "look at it!"

Cat looked. On Guy's palm sat the sculpture of a little owl. About three inches high, it was incredibly lifelike. Its feathers were articulated, yet stylized; the head was tipped, staring at something on the bird's right. The wings looked as if they were about to lift and the little owl was ready to take flight.

"That's incredible!" said Cat. "He just made that?"

"Yes," said Guy, still with a furiously sharp edge to his voice. "And he would have destroyed it if I had not prevented him, like those other four." He gestured at the clay pancakes on the table. "Cat, that's what has been going on. The boy is a sculptor, the most gifted clay sculptor I have seen in my life. That's what he's been using the clay for. That is why he does such a poor job of preparing it for my throwing work whenever I am gone!"

"Guy," Cat looked up at his scowling face, "why are you so angry at him? If he is a gifted sculptor, shouldn't he be sculpting?"

"YES!" shouted Guy, "yes, he should! He is misusing the clay, has been for weeks and weeks! I give him clay to prepare for throwing, and instead he makes brilliant figures out of it——animals, people, who knows what else—and then he *destroys* the work his gift and the clay tell him to make and haphazardly slaps it back together into a throwing body! It's no wonder I can do nothing with the clay after he misuses it like that! It's an outrage, a calamity! If I get hold of that boy..."

Suddenly Cat felt as if something had punched her, hard, in the chest. A sense of panic took hold of her. Something was terribly wrong—something with Andy.

"GUY!" she shouted at him, "you have to find him, NOW!" She took her husband by the shoulders, turned him around and gave him a push towards the door. "Run! Find him before it's too late! Go! Go! In the Wald, towards the Arbour, GO!"

Guy gave her a startled glance, then quickly, carefully, put the soft clay owl on the table.

"The Knowing?" he asked, briefly.

"Yes, YES, The Knowing! I don't know what is happening, but you need to find him! Go, GO!"

He yanked open the door and took off into the forest at a run.

CHAPTER 20

C AT FOUGHT DOWN THE panic in her throat. She had no idea what was happening, but she knew it was bad. What could she do? What did she need to do?

Water. They needed hot water. She ran back into the cottage, snatched up the kettle, rushed back out to the pump, filled the kettle brimful with fresh water, and dragged it back inside. *Hurry, hurry!* the voice inside her commanded. With a clank, she pulled up the burner cover and slammed the kettle into its place. Some of the water splashed out and steamed off with a hiss. *Two more sticks of wood into the firebox, blow on the flame as hard as you can*—where were the bellows? There, beside the stove, where they always were. *Calm down, Cat,* she commanded herself, *settle down. You need your wits about you.* She fanned the fire to a roar, clanged the firebox door shut, and drew a deep breath. What else? Cloths, some clean cloths. For bandages. And whichever of the herbs in her medicine chest were needed for injuries. Injuries? Was the boy injured?

Cat wished with all her heart Aunt was there. And then she was—Ouska and Uncle both stepped through the door into the cottage. Cat almost cried with relief.

"What is it?" Ouska asked curtly, not wasting time with greetings.

"Andy, the boy," Cat answered in the same tone. "Guy lost his temper at him for something he's done, and he ran into the Wald. Something is badly wrong. Guy went after him."

"I'll go see," said Uncle, and, without waiting for an answer, pulled open the door to go after his nephew and his apprentice.

"Towards the Arbour!" Cat called after him. He waved a hand in acknowledgement and disappeared around the corner. His wife shut the door after him.

"You think the boy's hurt?" she asked Cat. "I knew there was something wrong in the family, that's why we came, but I cannot feel more than that. I knew we would need Uncle, however."

"I'm so glad you're here!" said Cat. "I think the boy might be injured—there is some evil at work here, I don't know what. I started the kettle, and here are the cloths for bandages—but which medicines do we need?"

"What kind of injuries, do you think?"

"Bone, and skin. Boneknit, comfrey, basil?"

"Yes, and garlic. Do you still have any garlic oil?"

"I probably do, but I can't take the smell of it without throwing up. Here, it's in the chest." Cat reached up on top of the box bed and took down a small carved box, which she handed to Ouska.

"Yes, you have everything there. Camomile, too. Well done. Ah, you have marigold oil, that's as well; we can leave off the garlic then. We'll want a blanket, as well."

"Probably best his own, from his bed in the corner of the workshop," Cat said.

They took the medicine box and the cloths with them into the workroom and put them on the table. Cat threw an anxious glance through the window.

"Here!" she cried suddenly, "they found him!" She pulled open the workshop door. Guy and Uncle were coming towards the house from the path through the woods, half carrying, half dragging the boy, their arms reaching under his armpits and linked across his back. With their other hands they were supporting his upper arms, keeping him upright, as he was dragging his feet, sometimes trying to stumblingly put one foot in front of the other. As they came closer, Cat saw that the boy's hands were a horrible, bloody mess.

"Oh my God, Andy!" She pulled the door open as wide as she could and got out of the way as they dragged him across the threshold. Ouska, practical as ever, was bringing the heavy kitchen chair from the cottage; Cat sprang for the blanket and wrapped it around Andy's shoulders as the men lowered him gently into the chair. The boy was shivering convulsively and had a blank, catatonic stare in his eyes.

"What happened?" she asked Guy, her eyes wide. "Why are his hands in such a state?"

"He was hammering at them with a rock," said Guy, his voice shaking and out of breath. "When I found him, he was trying to smash at his left with the other, which was already a bad mess. It's like he was under some kind of horrific compulsion; I had to throw him to the ground and pry the rock out of his hand. He almost got me on the head with it, too." He wiped the back of his hand, stained with Andy's blood, across his forehead, leaving a broad smear. "If it had been in his left, his working hand, I'd be out cold in the forest right now. Again. Right by the clay pit, too, just like last time. I eventually got it from his grip, and he went limp. I was trying to carry him, but then Uncle came, thank goodness."

Ouska was bringing the kettle and a jug from the cottage. She poured some boiling water from the kettle into a large brown pottery bowl with camomile flowers in the bottom. "Get me some cloths," she said, "we need to try to clean his hands up a bit before we can see what we can do." She added some cold water from the jug to the bowl, then soaked the cloths in the camomile brew and wrung them out. "Here," she said to Cat, passing her one of the cloths, "let's try this. Help hold him, will you?" she said to her husband.

Uncle stepped behind the chair and closed his big hands around Andy's shaking shoulders. The boy sat slumped, staring at the floor in front of him, trembling and shivering.

Cat reached for his hand, carefully, expecting him to pull away. But the boy was limp and unmoving. Gently, Cat and Ouska wrapped the cloths around his hands, soaking up the blood, patting it off the backs of the hands and the mangled fingers.

"Why, Andy?" Cat asked, looking up into his black eyes with tears in her own, "why did you do this to yourself?" His stare was unresponsive.

They cleaned off the worst mess as much as they could, then wrapped his hands in fresh cloths with the herbs and oil. He shivered unabated.

"Can we warm him up somehow?" asked Guy, who had washed the blood off his hands and face and stood with his hands leaning on the table. "A cup of brew?"

"Yes, good idea," said Cat. "Get the Septimus cup; it's in the green box on top of the bed. And a bit of applejack?" She looked questioningly at Ouska.

"Just a little, though," said Uncle, "if you're giving it to him in that infernal blue cup. Knocking him out won't do much good."

They brewed a cup with valerian, lemon balm, and camomile and added a dash of the potent alcohol. With a splash of cold water, so as not to scald him, Cat put the cup to the boy's mouth. "Come on, Andy," she said, "take a sip, please!"

"I think you'll have to tip it right into him," Ouska said. "He's not responding."

"Here," Cat said, "can you...?"

Ouska stepped beside the chair, put one sturdy brown hand behind Andy's head, and with the other forced the edge of the cup between his lips. His teeth chattered against the rim of the dish. She poured the drink into his mouth, a little bit at a time. He gave a small cough, then swallowed. Some of the brew dribbled down his chin; Cat reached for a cloth to wipe it up, but Guy had forestalled her. Gently he dabbed the spilled drink off the boy's face and neck.

"Guy?" Cat said, when most of the warm brew had gone into the boy, "Guy, you need to try."

"Yes," he said quietly, "I do. It's my fault again——I need to try."

"No!" exclaimed the two women in unison. "It's not your fault, Guy," Cat said, laying a hand on her husband's shoulder and looking up into his eyes. "Don't think that. You were angry with him, but it's not your temper that made him do this. Your anger was *for* him, you were angry because he misused his gift. You want to see him using it right. This—this is something *against* him, something that is trying to stop him, to harm him."

"Listen to your wife, boy," his aunt said curtly, "she has it right. This is not your doing. But you need to use your gift to help the boy. If nothing else, because he's bound to you, you're his master. Try it, try putting your hands on him; I think you can do some good."

"I'll try," he said, his face serious. "But——I need you to hold him. He fought like a fury, just then in the Wald; there is no telling if he will not do so again when I touch his hands."

Uncle stepped behind Andy and laid his hands on the boy's shoulders. Cat knelt beside the chair on the left, put one hand on Andy's shoulder, the other on his lower arm, and Ouska did the same on his right. The boy showed no sign of even feeling their touch. His violent shivering had let up; he was now merely trembling softly, but his stare was still just as blank, directed at the floor in front of him.

Guy squatted down in front of the boy, directly in the line of his fixed look.

"Andy," he said softly, "Andy, son. I am sorry I shouted at you. I'm sorry." The boy's stare looked right through him. Guy reached out his hands, and carefully, feeling his way, placed his fingers on top of the boy's bandaged hands. There was no reaction. Guy felt with his fingers, as if he was trying to read the sensation, the back of Andy's hands, then slid his own hands over the boy's until his long, slender potter's fingers completely covered the others'. Cat felt a tension building in Andy's arm.

Guy gently, lightly picked up the boy's hands in his own, then placed them palm to palm, enclosing them in his hands. He closed his eyes, and his eyebrows drew together once more in that look of intense concentration. The tension rose.

Suddenly the boy's body arched in a tremendous spasm. Guy was flung back on his heels; Cat and Ouska tightened their hold on the boy's arms, but it was Uncle's strong hands on his shoulders that prevented him from lifting clean out of the chair. A groan came deep from Andy's chest, and his eyes rolled back in his head. A convulsion shook him from head to foot, and then he went utterly limp again.

"Evil!" Guy spat out. "There is a horrible evil in him!" He balanced himself back on his feet. "I was reaching into him," he said, "and then there was this dark, awful thing that sprang out at me——at him. What *have* they done to you, son?" His turquoise eyes looked up into the boy's face. The black eyes, half closed after the convulsion, opened again, in the same blank, desolate stare.

Guy looked at his aunt, then his wife. Cat returned his gaze.

"Yes, try once more," she said in answer to his unspoken question. "We have to try. Perhaps there is some way to get through."

They took up the same positions again, and Guy reached for the boy's hands.

"Andy, son," he said, "where are you?" Once again he ran his fingers over the boy's hands, slid them over the bandaged, mangled fingers, and Cat felt herself tense up in anticipation.

Suddenly there was a pattering of little feet, and a small body pushed itself between Cat and Guy.

"Andy owie!" said Bibby. She ducked between her father's arms, and laid her hands on Andy's knees. "Up!" she said. Cat and Guy exchanged a startled glance. "Bibby yit wif Andy!" said the little girl. Guy lifted the boy's hands from his thighs, and Bibby scrambled up on his lap. "Andy owie?" she said again, looking up into his face and patting his cheek with her chubby little hand. Then she turned her head and fixed her father with an imperial look. "Andy owie, Bubba make better!" She turned back to the boy, then suddenly flung her arms around his neck and pressed her red curls against his black head.

"Now!" shouted Ouska and Cat together, and Guy once again cupped the boy's hands, palm to palm, between his, and he turned the full force of his concentration into his hands. A shudder ran through the boy's frame, another, and another. Then a deep raspy breath came from his throat, and his body relaxed. But it was not the limp state of dead weight it had been before; Cat could feel that this was different.

Bibby loosened her hold on his neck. "Andy better now?" she asked. Four deep sighs came from the adults, and only then did Cat realize that she had been holding her breath. She released her hold on Andy's arm.

"Well?" she asked Guy. He gently laid the boy's hands back on his knees and looked into his face. Andy's eyes were closed and his head drooped, but it was more as if he was sleeping, not the catatonic state he had been in before. "I'm not sure," said Guy, "but I think *something* happened. Can we get the bandages off?" He lifted Bibby off Andy's knees. Cat and Ouska unwrapped the bandages around the hands.

"Yes, something happened here," Cat said. "This isn't cured, by any means, but far better than before, as if it had been healing for a week or two. I think even the broken fingers are beginning to mend."

"Yes, that's what I felt," said Guy. "I could not get far, but that black evil that prevented me from touching him at all at first was held back a ways this time." He laid a hand on Bibby's head. "Thanks to you, Karana." He smiled at her.

"Andy better?" asked the little girl.

"No, not all the way, but much better now," he said. "We must be good to him."

"Bibby dood to Andy," she said, "wight, Mumma?"

"Yes, you're very good to Andy," Cat said with a smile. "Let's get him into his bed so he can rest."

They carried the boy to his pallet in the corner of the room, and left the men to strip the wet, bloody clothing off him and get him into dry things. He remained fast asleep throughout the whole.

"He'll do for now," said Ouska, dumping the bloody water from the bowl out the front door and filling the dish with clean water to rinse the cloths. "There is something mighty peculiar about all this, though. Some dark force has a grip on that boy."

"There always has been," said her husband, coming into the cottage together with his nephew. "Just that he won't speak, that tells you right there. There's something holding him back, something that has a stranglehold on him."

"It's a dark thing," added Guy, who had carried the soft clay owl with him, "deep, dark, and evil. Nasty, slimy evil. The force of it was incredibly strong; it ripped right through me. I cannot imagine what it must feel like for him."

"Like an electrical shock, probably," said Cat, "you know, being struck by lightning."

"Yes," said Guy, looking at her curiously, "just like that. It felt just like those quick shocks you sometimes get from wool cloaks, but much, much stronger. It's deep in him, whatever it is."

"And I think," said Cat slowly, looking at the clay owl in Guy's hand, "I think it's been forcing him to destroy his pieces. His gift is so strong, he cannot keep himself from using it, but, somehow..." she tipped her head sideways, listening to something inside of her, "yes, somehow he is forbidden from making these things. That's why he always destroyed them as soon as he heard someone coming. But this time—this time you prevented him! So then this, whatever it is, this evil force in him, that curse, it made him try to destroy *himself*, made him strike at his hands, at the seat of his gift. Don't you think so?" she asked Ouska.

The older woman smiled. "I do not know, girl," she said, sounding curiously proud, "my Knowing tells me nothing of the boy. But it tells me of you, and that you're right in your own Knowing, that it does. Well done, girl." Cat blushed with pleasure at this compliment from her mentor, and Guy gave her a fond, proud look.

"I'm putting this on the drying shelf," he said, indicating the little owl. "Or, wait—it had best go in one of the cupboards, the locked ones. I would hate to have whatever beast is inside the boy find this little thing when he wakes up and try to destroy it then."

"No," said Cat, "that would be bad, I can tell. We need this. Here, go put owl in that pierced black walnut box on top of the bed, the one that had potpourri in it. It's empty just now, and Andy never messes with anything in the cottage. Inside the box, owl should be able to dry well enough, don't you think? And I need some mintbrew now, I do! Anyone else?"

"Yes, please!" everyone chorused, and Cat went to put the kettle on the fire.

CHAPTER 21

A NDY SLEPT SOUNDLY ALL the rest of that day and through the night. By the next morning, the sun was shining brightly, although the temperatures were well below freezing. The boy appeared in the cottage as Guy was cooking their breakfast porridge.

"Morning, son," said the potter, "how are you feeling?"

Andy gave his characteristic little shrug, then tried to pick up the water bucket to take it outside for filling as he usually did. He flinched hard and dropped the handle.

"Let's see those hands of yours," said Cat. "I don't think you'll be ready to carry anything yet for a while." She made him sit on the bench by the table and unwrapped the bandages from around his hands. "Well, it's looking better—far, far better than I would have expected after yesterday—but it'll take a while to heal completely. You'll have to take it easy and take care of yourself."

"Andy take care woozhelf!" repeated Bibby, climbing on the bench beside him and peering at his hands. "Andy owie!" Cat caught her pudgy hand just in time before she patted the boy's "owie" fingers.

"Don't touch Andy's hands," she said, "that would hurt him. But you can get me the medicine box from the shelf, sweetie, all right?"

"Med'zin botz?"

"Yes, from the shelf. The brown box. Let Papa get it down for you."

She re-bandaged the boy's hands with ointment and herbs.

"Guy—any suggestion for how Andy can hold a spoon? Else he's not eating much breakfast, unless you want to feed him."

Andy gave her a startled look from under his eyebrows, and she laughed at him.

"No, don't worry, we won't make Master Guy spoon-feed you," she said, "but it would help to rig something. Wait, I have an idea!" She took another strip of cloth, wound it around the outside of the bandages on his left hand, then took one of their carved wooden spoons and carefully slipped it into the fabric, so the handle of the spoon was held to his palm while its bowl protruded past his fingers. "There!" she said, proudly, "won't that work?" He gave his shrug, accompanied by a tiny almost-smile.

Guy was ladling out the porridge. "Come on, Bibby," he said, reaching down to put her on the bench for eating. Then he pulled up short. "What on earth are you doing, babe?"

"Bibby poon wike Andy!" said the little girl, with another strip of cloth bandage in her hand, trying without success to wrap it around the other hand. Guy and Cat laughed out loud, and Bibby's lip began to wobble.

"There, sweetie, don't cry," said Cat. "You want a spoon tied to your hand like Andy? Sure, why not. Come here, Mama will do it for you." She securely wrapped the bandage around Bibby's little hand, tucked in the end, and then pushed a spoon into the fabric folds. "There you are." She put the little girl on the bench beside the boy.

Bibby looked up at Andy with a wide smile and waved her spoon at him. "Bibby Andy poon!" she crowed. He looked down into her bright turquoise eyes, and an answering smile spread over his own face—a very small, but real, smile, a look which no one but Bibby ever got from him. He waved back at her with his own spoon.

"Well, I feel downright left out," said Guy, grinning over their heads at Cat, "but I think I'll stick with holding my spoon the old-fashioned way." Cat could see the relief in his eyes at the boy's quick recovery in mind as well as body. She fervently agreed.

After breakfast Guy took Andy outside.

"The boy needs to have something useful to do," he said to Cat on the way out. "I don't think he will be wedging clay for some time, which is perhaps as well. I want to be very careful to see what happens when he picks up the clay again for the first time. I very much hope his hands have not sustained any permanent damage; it would be a crime if they had."

"A crime is exactly what has been going on there, I suspect," said Cat. "Something or someone has been after him to do him harm, not accidentally, but actively and maliciously. I think he brought this with him when he came to Isachang."

"What do you mean, when he came to Isachang?"

"I think he is an Outlander, like myself—but not from my world, from another somewhere. With all I've been reading... But never mind that now. Go do some work."

CHAPTER 22

I T WAS A COUPLE of weeks later—that very morning they had unloaded the kiln, and the pieces were stacked on the table in the workshop and on the shelves above Andy's bed in the corner of the workshop. The little owl had come through the firing intact; Guy had slipped it in at the last minute, when Andy hadn't been watching, and it was the first thing he took out when he opened the kiln. The little sculpture was safely tucked away again in the potpourri box on top of the bed.

It hadn't snowed for a few days; the snow lay about two feet deep, but the space around the cottage and the path to the village were well cleared. Cat unloaded her basket: another book Nikor had found for her (she would have to take back the other two she was finished with, there was no more room on the shelf by the fireplace), two small loaves of sweet bread from Yldra, and some russet apples from Ouska's garden. Guy and the kids would enjoy the bread; Cat had not yet learned to bake pastries in her oven. And once the sweet bread was gone, there would be the apples for dessert. Maybe they could make some baked apples later on.

Cat yawned. She was becoming quite used to taking naps right along with Bibby; sometimes the little girl even woke up before she did herself. She was often sleeping like a log now, a quite different quality of sleep than her nighttime sleep or how she slept when she normally had naps. Usually, these sleeps were dreamless; she had not even had one of her radio dreams of Sepp, Nicky, and Ben in some time.

It burst in on her almost as soon as she closed her eyes.

A fist hammering against a door. Nicky's voice, frantic.

"Sepp, SEPP, open up, quick, OPEN THE DOOR!"

The sound of a door crashing open against the wall. Harsh, gasping breaths, interrupted by coughing, choking.

"Nicky! What on earth—quick, bring him in! What in blazes happened to his hands?"

The door slamming shut again, the sound of the dead-bolt being shot into place.

"Tyrone—the bastard, he caught up with Ben, out in the back alley behind the shoe store—he caught him, and Sepp, oh the bloody, bloody bastard! He was slamming Ben's hands in the steel door—Ben was already almost passed out with choking—I hit the bastard with the bag with the boots in it, hard—I think I knocked him out for a second so we got away—but Sepp, Ben's hardly breathing, and the rat's coming after us! What do we do, Sepp? What do we do?"

"Nicky, it's time. We need to go, now!"

"What do we do then?"

"The bowl, bring over the bowl." Rapid footsteps, clatter-ing sounds.

"Ben can't touch it, look at his hands! And he's barely conscious!"

"You will have to, then. There, I've got it unwrapped. Now help me get Ben over my shoulders. If I hook my arm around his leg I can hold him by the arm."

"SEPP! I think that's him on the stairs! Hurry, HUR-RY!"

"Quick then, quick! Pick up the bowl with the cloth and give it to me—with the CLOTH! Not with your hands, not until I tell you!"

Sounds of banging at the door, shouting, crashing. A rhythmic pounding, as if someone was ramming the door with their shoulder.

"SEPP! He's coming!!"

"Nicky, listen! I'll put my arm around you, and when I say so, you touch the bowl with your bare hands, and we'll hope to God it works. Hey, what are you doing?"

"The owl, I need my owl! There—now?"

"NOW!"

The sound of the door crashing open with a grinding, splintering noise.

Silence.

Cat jerked upright on the bed, her heart pounding, her eyes wide with fear. This was happening *now*, that mo-ment! Nicky and Sepp, in danger—where were they, wh at... No, it had not happened yet, not quite. Her sleep-ad-dled mind cleared, but the fear remained. It was extremely close, would happen very, very soon—and suddenly she knew. She threw back the blanket, pushed open the bed doors, swung her feet out of bed, and jumped up.

"Guy!" she yelled, "Guy!"

He ran from the workshop.

"What? What is it?"

"Guy, the Arbour, quick! Run to the Arbour! It's Sepp and Nicky—they need us! Go, run, RUN!"

He barely waited to hear her out, snatched his cloak from the hook by the door, and ran out the door.

Bibby, on the bed behind Cat, started crying.

"Mumma!"

Cat spun around, and snatched her up in her arms.

"It's all right, sweetie, I'm here, it's all right——shush, shush. Shh. That's better. Shush." Andy—where was Andy? He could stay with the little girl. She called out, but got no response. "Andy? Andy!" she called again through the door into the workshop, but he was not there. The sense of urgency in her pushed her hard. She took a deep breath and sat the baby back on the bed.

"Sweetie," she said, looking into the little girl's eyes, "sweetie, Mama has to go outside really quickly, Mama has to help Papa. Can you stay here? Please, just stay in the bed, okay? Mama will close the doors, and you'll be safe. I'll be back as quick as I can, but I have to go help!"

"Help Bubba? Help Unca Yepp?"

"Yes!" Cat nearly shouted, "yes, help Papa and Uncle Sepp! Oh bless you, sweetie, for your Knowing! Can Bibby stay here, can you do that for Mama?"

"Bibby tay."

"You're the best." Cat pressed a quick kiss on the little girl's cheek, then closed the bed box doors, pushed her feet into her moccasins, pulled her cloak from the hook, and rushed out the door.

She ran into the Wald, the path that led away from the cottage in the opposite direction from the village. It was a narrow lane that wound through the dense trees of the forest. Hurry, hurry! Cat's moccasined feet slipped on the snow. Not now, she needed to hurry!

But there! Around the bend, just past the clay pit, they came towards her. Sepp, supporting Nicky, darling Nicky, pale and frightened-looking, limping heavily and gasping, out of breath. And behind them, Guy, carrying—

"Andy?" said Cat, incredulously. "Again? His hands? What..."

"Cat!" Nicky gasped out, "Cat, you're here!"

Cat hugged her, quickly. "Yes, I am, but let's go, get home—here, lean on me—put your arm over my shoulder. Sepp, we can almost carry her between us; if we move sideways, she can hop—did she hurt herself?"

Her brother-in-law gave her a brief nod. "Twisted her ankle when we landed—we all fell, you know how it is."

The boy in Guy's arms was nearly unconscious, fighting for every breath.

They spoke no more until they reached the cottage and went in by the workshop door. Cat used her foot to pull out a stool from under the work table, and they seated Nicky onto it; Guy lowered the boy to a sitting position in the kitchen chair that stood in the middle of the room. The boy's hands were a bloody, mangled mess, and he was gasping with harshly laboured breaths. The horribly blank stare in his eyes sent an icy shiver down Cat's back.

"Mumma?" Bibby called from the next room.

"Yes, sweetie, we're here!" Cat called out. Then she turned to Guy, who knelt beside the chair by the boy. "What happened to Andy? Where was he?"

"Sepp had him, don't ask me why—I got to the Arbour just in time to see them arrive, in that whirling vortex from the bowl——you remember..."

"So the bowl worked for all three of you, then?" Cat asked her brother-in-law.

Sepp frowned at them, not listening.

"Ben," he said, "his name is Ben! Why—"

The back door swung open, and Andy stepped into the room. For one heartbeat, everything seemed to freeze into stillness.

Cat looked from one boy to the other. They were perfect mirror images of each other, identical black hair, black brows, long noses, brown skin. Andy's dark eyes swept the room, then fell on the boy in the chair. A shock wave seemed to run through him. He took a step, then another, moving like a puppet on a string; his arms came up, and he stretched out his hands to the other boy. His breathing became harsh, laboured. Cat's eyes went to the boy in the chair—Ben? This was Ben? A change had come over him, as well. His head was rising, his black eyes locked with the other's gaze. With the same puppet-like motion, he rose from the chair, took a step, and stretched out his hands. They met palm to palm, Andy's fingers interlacing with Ben's wounded ones. "A'verelm!" Ben gasped out, and Andy answered: "Br'oldyn…"

A spasm shook them, hard, and they staggered. Guy sprang up to support Andy; Sepp flung his arms around Ben's chest to hold him up. Another shock wave ran through the boys; their hands began to separate.

"No!" cried Cat, "no! Hold together!" She grasped Andy's left wrist, Ben's right, fighting to keep their palms pressed together. "Nicky, help me!" Her friend, moving as fast as her injured leg would allow, stepped up to the boys' other side, laid hold of their wrists and kept them steady. "Hold them," cried Cat, "we need to hold them together!" Shock wave after shock wave ran through the boys; their breathing became choking gasps.

Suddenly Bibby was between them. She flung her arms around Andy's legs, squeezed as hard as she could, then tipped back her head to look in his face.

"Bweave, Andy!" she commanded. "Bweave!!"

He responded as if under a compulsion, dragging a hard, gasping breath into his lungs, echoed by the same from Ben.

"Bweave!!" said Bibby again. "More!" The boys drew a second harsh, deep breath, then another, and another, deeper and more regular with each time. Then, suddenly, one more tremendous shock wave ran through them, their heads flung back, their backs arched, and they gave an inarticulate scream—then, at the same time, they dragged in a deep breath, blew it back out, and their bodies stilled. Their breathing smoothed out, evened, grew normal, until they stood, face to face, their hands interlocked, two pairs of wide eyes looking into each other.

Cat felt their hands relaxing and let go of their wrists; Nicky followed her lead. Bibby loosened her grip on Andy's legs, turned around, and grasped onto Cat's skirt instead. The boys' hands came apart, their knees buckled, and Guy and Sepp, in parallel motion, lowered them to the ground, where they remained sitting, gazing at each other.

"Now what in the *hell*," Nicky said, "was that all about?"

CHAPTER 23

C AT LAUGHED, THE RELIEF making her almost dizzy.

"Welcome to Ruph!" she said to her friend. "Drama is our specialty, provided free of charge to all newcomers. Guy," she said, turning to her husband, "Guy, their hands! Try it!"

Guy knelt down beside the boys, and reached out to Ben. "Let me see your hands, son—Ben, is it?"

"Br'oldyn," Andy said hoarsely, "Br'oldyn, my brother."

Guy turned his head and looked searchingly at his apprentice. "Andy?"

"A'verelm," said Ben, his voice the exact echo of the other's, "he is A'verelm."

Guy looked from one to the other. "A'verelm. Yes. Br'oldyn? May I—" He gently lifted the boy's injured hands in his. Ben flinched. "What happened?" asked Guy.

"Slammed in a door—" "Had a door slammed on him—" "Some creep hit him with—" Cat, Sepp and Nicky all spoke at the same time.

Sepp and Nicky stared at Cat.

"How do *you* know that?" asked Sepp. "Oh——the Knowing?"

"Well, sort of," said Cat. "I heard you, off and on, in the last few months. In my dreams. Like a radio play... Not very often, just sometimes. And I heard you just then, right before you came, when Nicky told you what had happened. It's how I knew to send Guy to the Arbour to meet you. And you see, Andy here—A'verelm?——he hurt his hands just like it, only a week or so ago—and Guy could not do much..."

"Guy?" asked Sepp with a puzzled look, "what would he be able to do?"

"Oh," said Cat, "I suppose you were gone by the time all that happened. We think it's part of his Septimissimus gift—watch!"

Guy had placed Ben's mangled hands together, palm to palm, and was cupping them with his own. His eyes closed; then he opened them again. "Sepp? He might need holding. Last time..."

His brother stood behind Ben, placing both hands on the boy's shoulders with a comforting grasp. Guy's eyes closed, and the now-familiar look of concentration came over his face. Ben's breathing grew shallow; then he pulled in one deep breath and shuddered from head to toe. His eyelids fluttered, his eyes rolled back in his head, and then he released his breath in one, big sigh. His lids opened, as did Guy's, and they looked into each other's eyes.

Guy slowly unfolded his hands, covered in the boy's blood, to reveal Ben's hands—dirty and bloody, but utterly whole.

Cat drew in a gasp, and tears shot into her eyes. She covered her mouth with her hands. "Oh Guy!" she said through her fingers, "oh, Guy!" He raised his head, and the look of wonder in his turquoise eyes sent a shiver down Cat's spine.

Guy laid Ben's hands back into his lap. The boy stared down at his fingers. "Holy crap!" he said, his voice cracking, "what just happened? And my hands look gross!"

Cat and Sepp laughed.

"More importantly, how do they feel?" Cat asked. "Can you move them?"

"Yeah, sure, why not?" he said, wiggling his fingers, "except—wait." He shook his head as if to dislodge something from his ear. "Wait a sec—" He looked around, looking disoriented. "Nicky—wasn't—hey, I can't remember——did I get a whack on the head? Wait, no—there was that guy—and he—" Suddenly he flinched, hard. "My hands, he—it hurt, it hurt so much—I couldn't breathe—and—" His disoriented gaze fell on the other boy across from him, and his voice changed again to the deeper timber it held before. "A'verelm——my brother..." He shook his head again and looked around wildly. "Sepp! Where—what..."

"Here, son. Right behind you," Sepp said, giving the boy's shoulders a reassuring squeeze. Ben slewed his head around to look at him.

"Sepp, what's happened to me?" His voice cracked in adolescent panic.

"It's all right, son, it'll be fine. You'll be all right." Sepp rubbed the boy's shoulders. "I don't know just what happened, but we will find out. It's all right," he repeated.

Cat had detached Bibby from her skirts and poured water into a bowl.

"Here, let's clean your hands," she suggested, gently. "You too, Guy. Your job isn't finished."

The water in the bowl turned crimson, but Ben's hands emerged in perfect wholeness, the brown skin over the knuckles unbroken, the fingers straight and smooth. Only faint scar lines on the backs of the hands gave evidence of the recent injuries.

Guy dried his hands on a towel, then turned to Andy.

"Come on, son," he said, "let me see yours." He looked at his brother. "Sepp?" Sepp nodded, then once again stepped behind the boy, who had stood up when Ben rose from the floor, and laid his hands on his shoulders. They were nearly of a height. *Andy is a bit taller than Ben*, Cat thought, *but not by much*. She stepped beside the boy and put her hands on his arm, just as she had held him the week before. Bibby ducked around her father, wrapped her arms around Andy's leg, and held on tight.

"Andy be better!" she said. He smiled down at her, then held out his hands to Guy.

Guy took them between his and looked into the boy's eyes.

"A'verelm, son," he said softly, "you can heal now."

And just like his brother, the boy shuddered and gasped; his eyes fluttered closed, then one tremendous spasm whipped through him as if a final hold inside him was ripping loose. He gave an inarticulate cry, shuddered once more, then grew relaxed and still. His eyes opened, and he looked up at Guy.

"Well done," said Guy quietly, "well done, son," and he opened his hands to release the boy's. The crusty scabs on the back of Andy's hands, an angry black-red only a few minutes before, were gone, in their place only faint white scars echoing those on his brother's knuckles. The brown fingers were once again straight and whole, all evidence of their horrible mangling gone.

"Andy all better!" Bibby cried triumphantly, turning her face up to the boy with a brilliant smile.

"A'verelm," said Cat, "his name is A'verelm, sweetie."

"Andy!" the little girl insisted. The boy smiled down at her, then looked up at Guy from under his eyebrows.

"Thank you, Master Guy," he said, in his hoarse adolescent voice, and he received a approving look from the turquoise eyes and a brief nod in response.

"You'll do, boy," said the potter. Cat smiled at how much he sounded like his uncle and aunt.

"Can somebody please tell me what's goin' on around here?" asked Nicky in a plaintive voice. She was hobbling over towards the chair, then suddenly lost her balance, came down too hard on her right foot, and cried out in pain. Cat sprang to her rescue, but Sepp got there ahead of her. He caught Nicky before she fell, then lifted her off her feet and set her down on the chair in the middle of the room.

"Careful, dear," he said with a concerned tone in his voice, and got on one knee beside the chair, bending to lift her foot.

"Ow!" Nicky cried, as soon as he touched her ankle. Her eyes filled with tears, and she bit her lip.

"Oh, Nicky," said Cat, "you poor sweetie! That foot's really bad, isn't it? Guy..." She turned to her husband, a look of appeal in her eyes.

Guy raised an eyebrow, then shrugged. "I can but try," he said, kneeling down beside his brother. He looked up at Nicky.

"May I?" he asked.

Sepp looked at him with a scowl. "Hey, don't touch her foot, she is really sore! I don't think you know what you are doing; we should wait until we can get help from Aunt. Nicky's had enough to hurt her!"

Two pairs of turquoise eyes locked, then Guy chuckled.

"Lay down your hackles, young 'un," he said. "I won't hurt your girl. I'll just put my hands on her foot; I promise to be careful. It can't harm her to try."

"Oh, very well," conceded Sepp not too graciously and took hold of Nicky's hand, as if he was trying to stake a claim. *All he needs now is to bare his teeth and snarl,* thought Cat, amused.

"Could you perhaps pull up your trousers a little?" asked Guy. "It would make it easier for me to lay my hands around your ankle."

Nicky reached down with her free hand and hitched up the leg of her jeans an inch or two, exposing a dirty white cotton sock and one of her blue canvas running shoes, soaked through from the snow. Even through the sock, Cat could see that the ankle was swelling up.

Guy bent low, reached out both his hands, and very gently laid them around Nicky's ankle. He closed his eyes and concentrated. The room had become still; nobody moved or spoke. A look of surprise came over Nicky's face, and Guy opened his eyes.

"Did you feel anything?" he asked, looking up at her.

"Yes! Yes, I sure did!" she said, looking from him to Sepp. Guy pulled his hands back. "It got, kind of, warm! And now it's feeling better. Still hurts a bit, but nothing like it did a minute ago! Wow! That's somethi—ah-ah-ahchoo!"

"Bless you!" said Cat automatically. "And bless *you*, darling," Cat said to Guy, pulling him up by his hand from the floor and giving him a proud look, "well done!"

"Wew done, Bubba," echoed Bibby, and everybody laughed.

Nicky sneezed again.

"Okay, that's it," said Cat, "you guys are soaking wet from rolling around in the snow! Let's make some brew—that's tea to you, Nicky—and get you warm!"

Nicky hardly limped at all any more, but Sepp still supported her carefully with an arm around her waist, although it was obviously no longer strictly necessary. Guy grinned at Cat over his brother's head. She waggled her eyebrows at him, with a significant look at the other two, and mimed a wolf whistle, which spread his grin even broader.

CHAPTER 24

"Miss Nicky," Guy said with exaggerated politeness, following Sepp and Nicky into the cottage, shepherding the boys along, "you are Catriona's best and long-lost friend?"

Nicky looked back at him over her shoulder, giving him a flirty smile through her bush of golden curls. Cat felt a momentary stab of jealousy, then laughed at herself for it. Not only was this Nicky, her best friend, who would never poach on another woman's reserve, but it was obvious by the way Nicky was clinging to Sepp's possessive arm where her interests lay. Sepp helped Nicky sit on the bench and settled down beside her, putting his arm around her shoulders.

"Oh, pardon me, I neglect my social duties!" Cat said, copying Guy's overly polite tone. "Miss Monica Bauer, may I present Dyniselm Septimissimus, town potter and mage, husband to your humble servant, Catriona Outlander?"

Guy made a leg, the elaborate bow that was reserved for formal introductions in Ruph, then took up the refrain.

"And may I present my young daughter, Ysbina Small-child?" He picked up Bibby and hung her upside down in front of the two on the bench. She squealed loudly, and he dropped her in his brother's lap. Sepp whipped his arm from around Nicky's shoulders to catch his niece.

"Unca Yepp!" the little girl squeaked and threw her arms around his neck. He laughed and cuddled her close.

Nicky stood up and dropped a curtsy, first to Guy, then to Cat. "Thank you, kind sir, for this welcome to your home, and to you, kind lady..." They dissolved into giggles, and Cat threw her arms around Nicky, rocking back and forth in a big hug.

"It's sooo good to see you!" she said, when they finally let go of each other. "I can't believe you're here!"

"I know! Me neither! I feel like—you know, it feels like I've got jet lag or something! I'm not sure I'm not dreaming, actually—well, it was a total nightmare at first, but now..."

"Looks like Ben isn't quite over the shock yet, either," said Sepp, looking at the boys standing awkwardly in the corner of the cottage. "Come on, son, sit. You too—A'verelm, is it?"

"Andy!" insisted Bibby loudly. "Andy yit! Ben yit too!" Andy looked at her from under his eyebrows with a half-smile, gave his little shoulder shrug, and slid onto the back bench. His twin, more shyly, followed suit.

"Sepp!" said Nicky, looking wide-eyed from him to the boys, "Sepp, the names! A'verelm and Br'oldyn—they sound just like Avril and Brolden! Is *that* why you couldn't

181

say those words, Ben—Br'ol—oh heck, I can't make myself say your fancy name! Can I just keep calling you Ben?"

"Okay," he said, giving a shoulder shrug almost exactly like Andy's—*except*, Cat thought, *he shrugs his right shoulder, Andy the left*. "I don't really know what's going on either, this is so weird..." His voice cracked again, and he gave a sidelong glance at his twin.

"Why don't we start the story at the beginning," said Cat, bringing some pottery mugs over to the table. Five—wait, no, there were six grown people, plus Bibby. She found two more cups. Guy followed her with the heavy brewpot, which like every other piece of crockery in the house was his own workmanship. They poured mint-brew for everyone, added a loaf of the sweet bread and a chunk of cheese to munch on, and settled around the table.

"Okay, the beginning," said Cat, looking at Nicky and Ben, "is probably three months ago, when I disappeared from Greenward Falls. Well, I guess just before that, when Sepp showed up there the first time. He went there and I came here the same way, with one of those bowls you've just travelled with. You know all about that, I suppose. And then I met Guy—actually, his name is really Dyniselm. He's something special—" she smiled at her husband, "well, he's the Septimissimus, the seventh son of a seventh son of a family who's really special to start with, the Septimus clan. That's why he's got those abilities you've seen earlier, and possibly some more; we don't know about all of them yet. But Sepp must have told you about that, didn't he?"

Nicky shook her head. "Not really. I guess I didn't want to hear it. Sorry, darlin'," she said to Sepp. "I should have listened."

He had his hand draped over her shoulder, and now lightly ran the outside of his thumb down her cheek. "It's all right, dear—I know it was hard to believe," he said. "But here we are, in Ruph. And here's my brother, and his baby girl, and—his wife?"

"You bet!" said Cat with a big smile. "It took us all of three hours after you left to get married properly, wedding chain and all."

He grinned his lopsided grin at that. "I knew that would happen," he said, "and now Bibby's got a new mama, eh?" He gave the little girl on his lap a little squeeze.

"Bubba Mumma!" Bibby told him importantly. "Bubba an' Mumma an' Bibby an' Andy!"

"That's right—Andy," Cat took up the tale. "He came to live with us a few weeks ago as Guy's apprentice. It was Bibby who named him Andy. Up until an hour ago, he never spoke one word himself. And I'm beginning to think I know why." Cat directed a questioning look at the boy.

"Yes, Mistress," he said in his hoarse voice, looking at her from under his eyebrows. "The power that bound me forbade me from speaking."

"Not just speaking, but more importantly, making what you are gifted to make, did it not?" said Guy.

"Yes, Master Guy. I was bound to neither speak, nor shape."

"Shape what?" interjected Sepp, with a look at his brother. "What does he work in?"

"Clay, of course. He's my apprentice, Cat told you. Why?"

"Because young Ben here is the most gifted wood carver I have yet to see. He…"

There suddenly came a gasp from Nicky, and she started frantically digging in her pants pockets. "My owl! Where's my owl? I had it in my hand, and then I touched the bowl, and I don't remember having it any more after everything went all swirly and we landed here and I twisted my ankle! Sepp, if that rat bastard made me lose my owl, I'm going to—" She looked like she was ready to cry.

"It's all right, dear. You probably dropped it when we fell in the Arbour," said Sepp, swallowing the piece of bread he had been chewing on. "I'll go see if it's there, shall I?" He rose from the bench.

"What's this you've lost?" asked Cat.

"My owl—a little carving Ben gave me for my birthday! I love it more than anything; it's beautiful. And Ben made it!"

"It's what I told you, Guy—the boy has a gift like none other I've seen," said Sepp. "I'll go look for the little thing; if it dropped in the Arbour, it'll still be there. Lend me your cloak?"

"Take Cat's," said Guy. "I'll come too. The more eyes to search, the better. Boys?" Andy and Ben slid out from behind the table and followed the men out into the snow.

The women looked at each other.

"Wow," said Nicky, "wow. I can't believe I'm here; I can't believe you've got a husband, and a daughter, and…

I can't believe all this is really happening..." She ran all ten fingers through her bush of curls.

"Nicky!" said Cat suddenly, "*what* is that on your finger? *Nicks*! Is that a ring? A *diamond* ring? On your *left ring finger*?? NICKY! I *knew* Sepp was perfect for you!"

Nicky had buried her blushing face in her hands, but now she peeped out between her fingers. "What makes you think it's from him?"

"Hah! As if it could be from anyone else! Let's see it, let's see!"

Nicky laughed and held out her hand for Cat to take a look at her ring. It was a dainty piece of jewellery, a plain gold band with one tiny diamond in a simple setting—but it was a diamond ring nonetheless.

"So, give, come on, tell! When did he give it to you, what happened?"

"It was just a couple of weeks ago, actually. Well, he asked me what people do in our world to get married—he did, I didn't hint or anything! So I told him that usually, you go have a ceremony in a church, or a Justice of the Peace's office, and that you have to get a marriage license. So he asked what you would need to get that, and I told him you had to take some ID to the registry office, you know, bring your birth certificates and stuff. And he looked kind of miffed at that—well, he hasn't got ID, of course. So then he asked if there was anything else people do, if the man gives something to the woman, and I told him the woman gets a diamond ring when they get engaged. And then a couple days later, he came home with this!" She waggled her finger, making the little diamond sparkle in the light. "And he asked me to marry him—and I said yes!"

"Oh Nicky, that's so awesome! But—hey, wait. What exactly did you both say? The precise wording, I mean."

"Oh, you're such a romantic! It was really classic, actually. 'Monica Bauer, marry me,' and I said 'yes,' and then he put the ring on my finger! And that was that."

"Aaaand—did he move into your bedroom then?"

"Get your mind out of the gutter! Well, yes, okay, he did. I mean, we're engaged, you know!"

"No, actually, Nicks—you're not just engaged. You're married! According to the customs here, that's how they get married! Except you don't get a ring, it's a necklace. See?" She pulled her silver necklace with the cat pendant out from under her blouse. "That's my wedding chain. Guy gave me that. And those words, that's what they say——'Marry me' and 'Yes, I marry you'. So when Sepp said that, he was marrying you, as far as he's concerned. Oh, Nicky! That means you're my sister-in-law!!"

Nicky sat with her mouth hanging open, then she closed it with a snap. "You've got to be kidding me! You've got to be—we're *married*? I think I have a bone to pick with that man! Tricking me into marriage under false pretenses! Just wait 'til I get my hands on him!" The wide smile on her face gave the lie to her indignant tone. "But hey, did you say sister-in-law? Eeeek..." They threw their arms around each other.

When they finally drew apart, Cat said: "This is so awesome! That means you're Bibby's aunty, too!"

"Aunnicky?" said Bibby now, who had sat quietly, watching all this with round eyes.

"That's right, sweetie," said Cat, "this is Aunt Nicky! She belongs with Uncle Sepp!"

"Aunnicky Uncayepp!" said the little girl, climbed up on the bench beside Nicky, and smacked a wet kiss on her cheek.

"Aww," said Nicky, "you're such a cutie!" and gave her a kiss back.

The door opened, and the men entered in triumphant procession.

"We found it!" Sepp called out, "we found it, just where we landed, in the Arbour! Ben was the one who spotted it; wasn't that clever of him?" He got down on one knee in front of Nicky and offered her the little wooden owl like a knight presenting a token to his lady.

"Oh, that's so great! Look, Cat, isn't this the most amazing thing you've ever seen? But, hey, you, *husband*," she took Sepp by the front of his shirt and pulled him up level with herself, "I just found out a very interesting thing from *my sister-in-law* here!"

"What?!?" said Guy, looking from the blonde woman to his brother, who was giving her a besotted and slightly sheepish look.

"Oh yes!" said Nicky, in mock outrage, "it appears that by the laws of this land, I am married to this man, when I thought all I was doing was agreeing to an engagement! Isn't that right, Cat?" She turned her head to look at her friend, but Cat had not heard a word Nicky had said. She was staring at the little wooden owl in her hand, turning it this way and that, and now held it out to Guy.

"Look! Look at this!"

Guy took the small sculpture, then looked at his wife. "You're right! It's just the same—no, wait." He reached up on the top of the box bed, brought down the small pierced potpourri box, and opened it. Out of it he took the little clay owl, and set the two figures side by side on the table.

"Well I'll be!" said Sepp. "They're exact mirror images!"

"Just like their creators," said Cat. Everyone looked at her. "Hadn't you noticed?" she said, "Ben is right-handed, Andy's a leftie! They do everything opposite from each other!" They turned to look at the boys and laughed. Ben's head was tipped to the left, listening in astonishment, his brother's to the right.

Something hooted outside.

"Heh, there's an owl," said Sepp. "Poor thing, we must have woken him up tromping around in the Wald; they're not usually out at this time of day." He picked up the two little owls and held them next to each other. The clay owl looked to the right, the wooden owl to the left. Their wing feathers looked as if they were ready to lift off in flight, the plumage ruffled by the wind. The live owl outside hooted again.

"Just look at this," said Sepp, "here, compare them!" He gave the clay owl to Ben, and the wooden one to Andy. The little sculptures sat on their palms, Ben's on his right, Andy's on his left. The boys gazed at the figures, and then, as if by a compulsion, lifted their hands until they were side by side and the two owl figurines touched.

Suddenly there was a tapping on the front window. They looked up to see a brown owl perched on the windowsill, peering into the room. It hooted loudly.

The boys startled, jerked their hands apart, and the little owl figurines fell to the floor. The owl at the window gave a derisive hoot, and took flight.

"What on earth..." began Guy, but Cat interrupted him.

"Wait, wait!" She picked up the little figures from the floor; the fall had done them no harm. She brought the two owls close together, touching them.

The owl's hoot sounded outside.

"Put out your hands again!" she said to the boys, and when they obeyed, she placed the two sculptures on their hands. "Now touch them together!"

Tap tap tap at the window, *HOOT!*

"Well I'll be!" said Guy. "I think we are onto something big here."

The candles were getting shorter and shorter in their holders, everyone's yawns longer and longer, when they finally bedded down for the night. They had just enough blankets to go around, one set to make a double bed roll on the floor for Nicky and Sepp, another to get Ben fitted up to bunk with Andy in the workshop. Cat smiled to herself, listening to the soft breathing and rustling of bedding in the room, and she slowly nodded off.

The dream unrolled itself in front of her eyes like a silent movie.

The quarry on the plains, in the dark—suddenly a shimmering, turquoise light, becoming a vortex, swirling, whirling. A figure appears in its centre, a man who staggers, falls. Then he picks himself up, slowly, and walks out onto the plains. The scene changes—he is on a horse, riding, riding through the night.

He's coming here, Cat thought, *he is coming for them...* then the image went dark. Cat woke, briefly. *That quarry,* she thought. *I have seen it before, in just such a dream. But when?* She drifted back to sleep before she could remember.

CHAPTER 25

NICKY HITCHED UP THE skirt that Cat had loaned her; it was a bit long and loose on her. They were walking to the village, to Sepp's place; he shared a house with one of his brothers, she had been told. One of five older brothers, other than Guy. Nicky liked this new brother-in-law of hers. She had never let Sepp tell her much about his life in Ruph—she just had not wanted to believe it—but he had kept mentioning Guy, anyway, almost as if he couldn't help it——and now that she saw them together, she knew why; the two brothers' fondness for each other was obvious. And so was the fact that the tall, red-headed potter was head over ears in love with Cat, who was fairly glowing with happiness in response. Nicky loved seeing it. Her head was still in a whirl from every-thing that had happened in the last twenty-four hours, but if it took being magically whisked off to another world for Cat to find happiness, then that was all right by Nicky. Guy seemed quite different from Sepp, but Nicky got that same vibe from him that she had had from her husband right from the first, that he was the genuine article—they were trustworthy, these men. Trustworthy, and reliable, and kind, and... She grabbed for the hand of Sepp, who was walking beside her, gave it a squeeze, and mimed a quick kiss at him. He smiled back, and tried to make it a real kiss while still walking, but a tree root protruding into the path tripped him up and nearly sent him sprawling.

"Keep your eyes on the road, man," said Guy from behind them, the smirk on his face obvious in his voice, "you've never been able to do two things at once. It takes talent, see?" Nicky looked around to see him lean over and give Cat an expert smooch while navigating the bumps on the path.

"No fair," Nicky said, "you guys have practise, and besides, you know this road. How much further is it?"

"It isn't," said Cat, as they went around a bend in the path, "look, there's the first houses. That's Aunt and Uncle's place there." She indicated a sizeable half-timbered house to the right of the road.

"Aren't they home?" asked Sepp, looking at the closed shutters. "Oh, no, of course not," he answered his own question, "they're out at the farm this time of year." He was still wearing the jeans, hoodie, and running shoes he had come from America with. Nicky was in a blouse and the blue-and-green-tiered skirt Cat had bought back in Greenward Falls, the only one of her skirts that wouldn't drag on the ground for Nicky. She still had on her jeans and runners underneath, but Cat had decreed that there was no point in making a bad first impression in the town by walking around in indecently snug trousers without a proper skirt to cover them up. Nicky giggled a little at that—'trousers'. Cat had been there only three months and was already starting to sound like she belonged.

Nicky looked around curiously. Ruph looked like the perfect medieval village—well, not perfect; *real*. The roads were hard-packed snow, probably just dirt underneath; half-timbered houses roofed in weathered wood shingles lined the lanes. If her reenactors' group could see this, they'd go crazy! She could hear chickens clucking from behind closed gates, and the smells told her that some of the backyards had a few other animals stabled in them as well.

They turned from the wider road down a narrow alley and stepped out into an open square.

"This is the marketplace," said Cat, "and there's my library!" She pointed at a big, Tudor-style building with a red tile roof and large carved double doors.

"*Your* library?" Sepp said, one eyebrow raised.

"It might as well be," said Guy, "half the town is starting to call her Catriona Bookwoman instead of Catriona Potterswife, as is proper." He gave Cat his lopsided grin.

"Well, I do love the... Hey!" Cat interrupted herself, "there's that guy again!" She pointed her chin in the direction of a low-eaved building on the opposite side of the square with a carved wooden plaque swinging from a beam over the door. An inn sign! Nicky secretly shook her head. Unbelievable. She had landed in a real-life Renaissance fair. She looked at where Cat was pointing and saw a black-haired man in a grey cloak, who had apparently just stepped out of the tavern.

"Remember," Cat said to Guy, "it's that strange fellow I told you about who scared me in the market that day Uncle and Andy came home. I thought he had gone—I *hoped* he had gone! What is he doing here?"

"Yoohoo!" came a high-pitched voice from their left, "yoohoo, Sepp! You're back!" A young girl with long dark hair, who was probably no older than in her mid-teens, sashayed up to them, hips swinging provocatively. She looked vaguely familiar, but Nicky couldn't quite place her. "Sepp!" the girl fluted, "how good to see..." Suddenly her eyes met Nicky's. Her exaggerated smile turned downward, her lips pursed and her eyes narrowed. Then she did a double-take, looked away from Nicky and Sepp to Guy, turned on the smile again, and fluttered her eyelashes.

"Hello, Kashinka," said Cat. Nicky was surprised at the edge in her friend's voice.

The girl's gaze met Cat's, the smile dropped altogether, and she frowned. "Oh," she lisped, "oh." Then she looked past them, and her attention was caught by the man in front of the inn. "Oh! It's Mosrim!" She swung around, whipping her long hair across her shoulders, and set out across the market. "He's so *charming*!" she tossed over her shoulder—it seemed directed at Cat, Nicky thought. With swinging hips, the girl went in pursuit of the dark man. "Mosrim! Yoohoo, Mosrim!" She caught up with him as he was turning the corner of the inn, and Nicky just saw her hooking her arm through his as they passed into the lane beyond it.

"Now what in tarnation was *that* all about?" she said. "And who is that? I almost feel as I've seen her before."

"Let me explain," said Cat. "I think I've got a pretty good idea what just went through sweet Kashinka's head. It probably went like this"—she pitched her voice in a breathless squeak—"'Ooh, there's Sepp, the Septimissimus! Ooh, great, he's back, so I can start hitting on him again! But ooh, hey, who's this chick on his arm? He's my guy, *I* want to marry the Septimissimus! But, ooh, Sepp's not actually the Septimissimus, so I don't really want him after all! Guy is the Septimissimus, ooh, and there he is! But, ooh, hey, he's taken by that outlander woman, drat her! But, ooh, there's that other stranger, ooh, I think he's a good bet!' And off she went," Cat added in her normal voice.

Guy and Sepp howled with laughter.

"I think you have her dead to rights," Sepp grinned. "As for why she looks familiar, Nicky, you're probably seeing the resemblance to her cousin, Ashya—Ashley, as you know her."

"Oh! Yeah, that's it," said Nicky. "I didn't spot it at first because she's dark, and Ashley is a blonde. Ugh. So I take it she's about as charming as her cousin?"

"Yes, pretty much," said Cat. "Not that I've met Ashya, but I've heard more than enough, and pardon me if I'm just a little prejudiced against her. And Kashinka certainly is the original airhead. But," she turned back to Guy, "what *is* that fellow doing here? I don't like him; he gave me the creeps last time! What did she call him—Muslin?"

"Mosrim, I think," answered Guy. "You know, I believe I've seen him around town in the last week or so; he's been here a while."

Suddenly Nicky saw a scurrying movement by the corner of the inn. Terror shot through her, and she gave a shrill scream. "Mice!" She darted behind Sepp.

"Where?" called Cat. Nicky was cowering against Sepp's back and waved a hand in the general direction of where she had seen the dreaded rodents. "Over there somewhere! I know I saw some!" she said, her voice muffled in Sepp's sweater. He reached behind himself, pulled her out, and wrapped his arms around her.

"It's all right, dear, I'll protect you from the menace," he said consolingly, a barely noticeable amount of amusement swinging in his voice.

"Don't make fun of me!" Nicky protested, covering her face with her hands and hiding it on his shoulder. "I hate those awful things! They persecute me!"

"You know, they do," said Cat; "somehow mice seem to come after Nicky. And there are tons of them around here right now. But it's okay, Nicks; I don't see anything over by the inn any more. Come on, let's get going and get you home to your own house; I'm sure Chelm has kept it mouse-free. He says his tabby is one of the best mousers in town."

CHAPTER 26

THEY WERE IN THE alley behind Cobbler's Row the following day, passing the end of Six Fishes' Lane. The other end of the small road opened onto the market; Cat could see the back of Yokan's fishmonger's stall from their end of the passage and, beyond that, the colourful market crowd milling about. A couple of shoppers were loitering behind the stall, deep in conversation.

"Look, Nicky, there's the market through there," said Cat. But her tour guide impression met with an unexpected result. Nicky looked down the lane, then gasped.

"Ben! It's him!" She grabbed the boy by the arm and dragged him around the corner, out of sight from the market. A simultaneous hoarse outcry came from Andy, and suddenly he was cowering in the snow heaped up in the narrow gap between two of the houses. Nicky and Ben stood pressed against the rough-plastered wall, pale and wide-eyed with shock.

"What?" Sepp took Nicky by the arm protectively.

"There!" Nicky whispered, fear constricting her voice, pointing towards Six Fishes' Lane, "it's him, it's rat face! He's come after us!"

Sepp stepped into the passage, took one look, then quickly moved back out of sight. "You're right, it's the vermin," he said. He clenched his teeth so hard a muscle in his jaw jumped. "Not only that, there's two more of them."

Cat and Guy looked down the lane. A third man had joined the first two, and an argument had broken out.

"Wait!" said Cat, "the one that just came is the black-haired guy! That Mus-Mosrim fellow! And who are those other two, the mouse-grey ones?" She hustled Bibby out of sight of the market. "Who are they, Sepp?"

"One of them is the Tyrone guy who was hounding Ben," said Sepp curtly, his hand curling into a fist, "the one who nearly killed him."

Guy bent down to Andy, who was trembling in the recess between the houses, his forearms flung over his head as if to protect himself. Guy laid a hand on the boy's arm. Andy started violently.

"Andy, son, what is it?" Guy asked. He put his arm around the boy's shoulders, and was ready with his other hand, catching the boy's arm as he struck out wildly. "A'verelm!" he said firmly, "look at me!" Andy slowly lowered his arm, and looked up at Guy, stark fear in his eyes. "Come, son," said Guy, "come. Don't be frightened." Andy's black eyes locked with Guy's for a few seconds; then he let himself be pulled to his feet.

"The master," he whispered, hoarsely, "the slave master!"

Ben's head whipped around at those words, and the fear in his pale face deepened.

"The slave master!" he repeated in the same terrified whisper, and Cat could tell that those words were the stuff of nightmares for the boy.

She drew a deep breath and took one more look around the corner down to the market.

"Let's get out of here," she said, "come on, now! They're fighting, they won't come this way. Let's go, come on!" She picked up Bibby and took Nicky by the arm. Sepp, after a glance at her, followed suit, putting his hand on his wife's back, pulling Ben with the other. Guy led Andy, and together they ran the last few steps to the back door of Sepp's house.

Slowly, piece by piece, over several pots of mintbrew, the story came out. As Andy spoke, haltingly, hoarsely, Ben seemed to remember more and more.

The slave master, Andy told them, was the man who had brought him to this world and then to Kaltbur's house in the city, the rat-like man who had bound the boy into apprenticeship to Guy's family. Andy had been tied by a curse, a curse that kept him silent and subdued, prevented from doing what his nature called him to do. "I know not," he said, slowly, "what manner of evil the slave masters wished on me, or why they hated me so. I was nought but a humble slave boy. My brother—" he stopped.

Ben took up the tale, his voice husky. "We were mere children, not more than five summers, when the slave masters tore us apart and gave me to the woman. They brought me to the sacred place, and there they commanded the woman to be gone with me and never more to be seen. They said she would be free. They gave her gold, but they charged her never to return or she would die. Then she grasped me in her arm, took up two stones of blue, and then... I forgot..." His voice cracked, and he fell silent.

"So," said Cat, "the two of you are from a different world—I think I know which one, I'll tell you in a minute. Now, your parents...?" The boys, their black eyes fixed on her face, shrugged. "You don't remember them? They probably died when you were little." Andy nodded. "So you were raised as slaves, by these slave masters? Then for some reason they decided to separate you. You, Ben, were sent to America with this woman, who called herself Verena there."

The boy had a frown on his face. "But..." he began hoarsely, "I don't..." He looked at Nicky for support.

"She did say she was your mother, that you were her kid," Nicky said, her forehead wrinkled in concentration, trying to make all this out. "And Charlie obviously believed her, or he wouldn't have adopted you. But perhaps she just talked him into it; it's possible, he was kind of gullible. It was believable enough, though, Verena had the same colouring as you—I thought you both were Mexican or East Indian or something. What were you and she doing before she hooked up with Charlie?"

Ben knotted his eyebrows, then silently shook his head.

"You don't remember much of anything, do you?" asked Cat. "It must have been part of the curse they put you under. As long as you were with her, you didn't remember." He gave a shrug and a slight nod. "She was probably another one of their slaves, and they paid her off in order to get rid of *you*. Does that make sense? And then she married Charlie Bauer, and when they were killed, that curse you were under began to break up and you started to remember small bits and pieces—but you couldn't speak of them, or you started choking."

"Of them, or anything to do with his old life," said Sepp. "His worst choking fits were when he tried to speak their names, Br'oldyn and A'verelm, or even something that sounded similar. And then of course when rat man came anywhere near him—the longer, the worse. Where does he come in, I wonder?"

"Well," said Cat, "my guess is that somehow these slave masters found out that Ben was starting to break free of the curse, and they sent this Tyrone, if that's really his name, after him. I heard something in a dream to that effect. Except that this time, it must not have been enough to move Ben to another world—they wanted to stop him by force. And I think that's what happened to you, too, Andy, isn't it?" The boy's head was tipped to the right, listening. "I think they moved you to our world here, had you brought here by one of theirs, then bound you as apprentice to a master so you would be unable to leave." He made some affirmative noises in his throat. "Except by then they had a better idea just how valuable you could be, so they put a much stronger curse on you than they put on Ben—a curse that ensured you would not speak at all, and that if you rebelled against your bond, did what you were driven to do and used your gift, and especially if someone saw you at it, you would destroy *yourself*." All eyes were on her, and the boys were slowly nodding their heads. "But they hadn't reckoned with Ruph, with the Septimus powers, and with the force of a small Unissima Maxima who knows what love is." Cat laid a hand on Bibby's red curls.

"So the curse is broken," said Guy.

"Yes," said Cat, "but I think the boys are not out of danger yet. You see, from what I heard in that dream, I believe that somehow they got wind of it that the two brothers are back together, and something is about to break. There were three rat guys there on the market, two with grey-brown fur—uh, sorry, hair, I mean—and another with black. Am I right that the slave masters, the ones you're afraid of, have brown hair—well, greyish-brown?"

"Yes," Nicky said, who had listened to all this with a thoughtful expression, "that Tyrone creep looks like a rat. All the way, including hair colour." She shuddered. "He's horrible."

"The slave master looks like vermin!" said Andy vehemently, then he pulled up short. "I—I must not speak with disrespect—Yes!" he said suddenly, and loudly, "*vermin*! The slave masters look like grey vermin!" He spat into the fire, making the flame hiss and sizzle.

Guy gave him a small, satisfied nod of approval.

202

Cat smiled at both of them. "Well, I thought as much. You see," she reached for her basket, and pulled out a brown leather-covered library book, "there's that other fellow out there. He looks like a rat, too, but his hair is black. You've all been saying these fellows are rat-like, rat faces, rat guys—and I agree, this one is just like a rat. But I think he's different, and not only in hair colour. I'm pretty sure that he's after you two, as well," she looked at the boys, "but for a different reason. Those slave masters, they want you destroyed. If they can't make you destroy yourself, they will try anything to do the job themselves." Cat opened the book about two-thirds through the volume and turned a few pages to find the right passage. "But if I'm right about this, the black one, he wants you whole, alive. And here is, I think, why (it's the tale of *The Rats of Chaelia*)—"

Andy and Ben gave a strangled outcry. Cat glanced at them.

"Yes, Chaelia is your country, isn't it? Everything I've read about it fits. According to the books—and correct me if I'm wrong—there has been a battle raging between two factions in that world, two tribes. They both call themselves the Rats; it's all in here. And now, listen to this:

"In the days of the Grey / there shall come a power / a power which harnessed / shall restore the glory /

"the glory of the ebony and night / a power of a like pair / which joined together will be one /

"brother to brother / hand to hand / the power shall rise / strike down the foe of the Black /

"and restore the glory / against which none shall prevail...

"and so on and so forth, all in the same vein," said Cat, closing the book. "So, you see, there's two groups, the Grey and the Black. Probably it refers to their colouring. And here is this prophecy with foretells the 'power of a like pair'. I have a hunch that you are that power, or at least they think you are. You're twins, 'a like pair', and you have that twin gift, the same ability in different form. That's why they want you—the one set wants you to use you, and the other will do anything they can, up to and including killing you, to prevent the first set getting a hold of you."

"Oh my," Nicky said. "That's... oh my! But what kind of power are we talkin' about here?"

"Well," said Cat, "I think we've got an inkling yesterday afternoon just what it could be."

"The owls?" asked Guy, and Sepp was nodding his head.

"Yes, the owls," said Cat. "Two gifted sculptors, making a mirror image of the same creature, which, when brought together, brings the creature to life, or calls it to you when you want it. You can make things happen with your hands, boys. Under the right influence, or the wrong, as it were, you could be a fantastic weapon. They want you."

"So," said Guy, with wrinkled forehead, "what does it mean?"

"It means," said Cat, "that unless we do something, the boys are going to be dragged off to their native world and be made to do the bidding of some power-hungry tyrant. Or, alternatively, they'll be made into mincemeat by said power-hungry tyrant's opponents. I can't say I fancy either solution. We need a plan."

CHAPTER 27

"THE HAPPIEST OF BIRTHDAYS, little cousin!" sang out Sepp, as he toasted Yldra with a cup of Uncle's best cider. "Happy birthday!" "Many happy returns!" echoed the other guests around Yldra's kitchen table. Uncle beamed fondly at his daughter and her husband at the head of the table, then set down his cup and let out a large belch.

"Father!" scolded Yldra with a laugh.

"Pardon my manners," said Uncle unrepentantly, "but you have only yourself to blame. Wasn't me who made the roast meat as good as that, and your honey cakes get better every year. Are those hedge nuts ground into that dough?" He reached for the plate in the middle of the table and helped himself to another one of the small round pastries.

"Oh, yeah, those are so good," sighed Nicky, "I wish I could eat another one! Like doughnuts, don't you think? But denser and richer, and not as sticky-sweet," she said to Cat, who sat across the table from her friend with little Bibby on her lap.

Andy and Ben sat silently at the foot of the table. Cat suspected that Ben was still unsure of himself in this new world, while Andy never spoke much to begin with, even now that he had found his voice. He probably felt shy about eating at the table with his master's family, including the formidable wisewoman and her husband, the brewmaster. But to make up for their silence, the boys had made bigger inroads into the feast meal than the grown men.

"And now," said Cat, "Bibby has something special she practised for Aunty Yldra!" She lifted the little girl from her lap, and stood her on the bench. "Remember, sweetie?" She mimed the first words of the song, and Bibby broke into the tune: "Happy birfday to you, happy birfday to you..." Cat, Nicky, and Ben joined her in the last line, and "Happy birthday to yoooou!" rang out to the applause of the whole company.

"Fine singing, Bibby," praised Yldra, "you'll have to teach us all, dear!"

"Get the oud, Lozyb," called Sepp.

"Yes, do," said Uncle to his son-in-law. "Here, I'll help you fetch the music."

They quickly returned from the next room bearing an assortment of stringed instruments and a large wooden box that clanked and jingled, obviously holding some rattles or other percussion instruments. Lozyb picked up a something that looked like a lute and began plucking the strings to see if it was tuned; Guy seized on a similar, though slightly smaller piece, and Uncle took a little fiddle-like instrument that nearly disappeared in his large hands. Ouska pulled a round-bellied clay flute from the box.

"Oh, look," said Nicky, her eyes shining, "is that an ocarina?"

"We call it a chun," said Ouska and blew a few reedy notes on the little pipe. "This one"— she pointed at Uncle's little fiddle—"is a rebec, and those are ouds."

Yldra picked out a round hand drum, like a tambourine without jingles. Bibby and little Randor were given small maracas, just the right size for their little hands, and they immediately started shaking them enthusiastically. Once the strings were tuned to the little clay flute, the musicians tried their hand at a rendition of "Happy Birthday to You", and after only two rounds they had the tune together. The harmonies they used were a little different from what Cat and Nicky were used to—they sounded more like the music at Nicky's medieval fairs——but it worked.

Then Uncle broke into a breezy fiddle tune, the younger men on the ouds and his wife falling in with the music. The others were tapping their toes or drums or shaking their rattles, and when the melody wound to a stop after several repeated rounds, Nicky clapped her hands. "This is too much fun," she said with a wide smile. "What else have you got?" She leaned over the big box and suddenly squealed with pleasure. "Look, Cat!" Triumphantly she pulled something out of the box and held it up. "A flute! Well, more of a recorder, really. May I?" she asked Yldra.

"Go ahead," the young woman said, "that's what it's for."

Nicky put the instrument to her lips and blew some notes up the scale and back down again. "Not bad," she said, "it's got a bit of a different tuning than I'm used to, but I think I can do something with this!" She went into a cheery little tune; Cat thought she recognized "Pop Goes the Weasel" with a few half-tones changed. Lozyb and Guy quickly followed her, picking out the chords as they went along. The children randomly shook their maracas with more energy than rhythm, and Cat tapped her fingers on the table and sang along. She was smiling at Ben and Andy, who were nodding their heads in time to the music, when she caught sight of a movement underneath the dresser on the other side of the kitchen. Was that...? Just then, the song ended, and whatever had been moving was gone.

"Play 'The Lady by the River'," said Sepp, and Uncle picked up the rebec and fiddled a lilting tune, which was picked up by the ouds and Aunt's little clay chun. Sepp struck up the lyrics in a clear tenor, and Nicky and Cat listened as the others joined in the chorus about the lady walking by the river biding for her love. Lozyb sang a deep bass counter-tune, and Yldra's soprano echoed above the main melody line.

"Oh, that's beautiful!" said Cat when the last few notes had faded away "It's a bit like 'Greensleeves', isn't it, Nicky?"

"Yes, it is," replied her friend. "Here, listen." She put the recorder to her mouth and piped the soft Renaissance tune. Cat started to sing the words.

"Alas, my love, you do me wrong to cast me off discou rteously..."

But the words nearly stuck in her throat. There was the movement under the dresser again! She tried to remember the lyrics and watch for the motion at the same time. She made it through the first stanza and the chorus, then let her voice trail off; the men had picked up the key and were accompanying Nicky on the ouds. Sepp, who sat beside Nicky on the opposite side of the table, had his chair turned sideways, facing his wife. He saw Cat staring between them under the dresser, and he followed her gaze.

Now Cat was sure of what she was seeing. Frantically, she kicked Sepp under the table, and when he turned to look back at her, gave him a very small warning shake of her head. *Whatever you do, don't draw attention to it!* she thought at him. *Nicky would freak out!* He gave her a small nod in response and started tapping his heel on the floor in time with the music—stomping, foot in, foot out, kicking as if he was dancing a Russian mazurka while still firmly seated on the chair. The mice skittered back under the dresser, but only for a second before they ventured out again, as if something was luring them. Cat broke into the chorus of the song again—anything to keep Nicky's attention away from what was happening behind her back. "Greensleeves is my delight, Greensleeves is my heart of mould, oh, who but by Lady Greensleeves," she warbled.

Nicky broke off her playing and burst out laughing. "Heart of *mould?*" she crowed.

Cat was confused. "What? Oh!" She laughed, too, and out of the corner of her eye she saw that the mice had vanished again. "Gold, I meant, heart of *gold*! That's hilarious."

The Ruphians had struck up another tune with chun and rebec. Cat listened with only half her attention. There was something gnawing at the back of her mind. Flutes. Mice. Something she had read very recently, something that reminded her of an old story, something... Suddenly it clicked.

"Okay," she said, when the piece of music was finished, "I have a weird idea. There's something I want to try. Nicky? I want you to stand on your chair, close your eyes really tight, and play us a tune."

"Huh?" said Nicky, "what's that supposed to be in aid of?"

"I'll tell you afterwards, when I know if it worked. Come on, humour me, please?"

"I don't know—what if I fall off when I have my eyes closed?"

"Sepp can hold you; right, Sepp?"

"Oh, all right, if I must," said her brother-in-law with a grin. "Come on, dear, up you get." He helped his wife climb onto the chair she had been sitting on and placed his hands firmly at her waist.

"Okay, ready, set, go!" said Cat.

Nicky rolled her eyes at her, then pinched them shut and put the flute to her lips. "*Three blind mice, three blind mice...*" the tune rang out.

Cat circled her finger in the air to tell the others to pick up the tune, then pointed to the dresser, pressed her finger to her lips, and shook her head at them so they would not let on what they were seeing.

Several little grey mice crept out from under the cupboard and skittered closer and closer to the chair Nicky
was standing on. Yldra sucked in her breath in a gasp of
disgust (*thank goodness the music is covering the sound*, Cat
thought); Ouska drew back as if she was getting ready
to throw something at the vermin. One mouse after the
other scuttled out from under furniture, from corners,
and underneath the wood stack by the stove, and one
even squeezed its way under the gap of the closed bedroom door, until a round dozen of them sat in a circle
around the chair, rearing up on their little hind legs and
stretching their paws towards Nicky as she played the tune.
She stopped playing. The mice scuttled back under the
furniture; in less than a second not a rodent was in sight.

Nicky opened her eyes. "So?" she said.

"One more time, okay?" Cat said, "Please."

"Oh, fine," said Nicky, resigned, closed her eyes and
played.

"*Hickory dickory dock, the mouse ran up the clock...*"

The mice crept back out, and gathered around, scrabbling at the legs of the chair as if they wanted to climb it.

"Mousies!" called Bibby excitedly.

Nicky's eyes popped open. She let out an ear-splitting
shriek, and threw the flute at the rodents. They skittered
for cover, and Nicky burst into tears. Only Sepp's hold
on her waist kept her from falling off the chair; now she
collapsed into his arms and sobbed.

"How could you?" she cried at Cat. "How could you do
that?"

Sepp gave Cat a dirty look. "Yes, why?" he asked.

"Aunnicky pay fute an mousies come out!" said Bibby.

"Yes, exactly," said Cat. "Aunt Nicky played flute and mousies—I mean mice—came out. Look, Nicks, I'm really sorry; I didn't want to freak you out. But I had to know for sure. At least I made you stand on the chair so they couldn't reach you—I know how they bother you!"

Nicky sniffed. "I hate them!" she said, in a choked voice. "Why? What's going on?"

"Monica is a Piper, isn't she?" said Ouska.

"Yes, I think so," replied Cat. "You know about this?"

"There have been stories," said the wisewoman, "none in recent memory, but from the long past. But go on, you know something, do you not?"

"Yes," said Cat slowly, "yes, I know something. Nicky," she turned to her friend, "where did your family come from? I mean your ancestors, your grandmother and grandfather. Didn't you tell me..."

Nicky sat with her feet pulled up under her skirt on the seat of the chair so she would not have to touch the floor; Sepp's arm was wrapped around her, his other hand rubbing her back. She glowered at her friend. "Germany, I guess," she said with another sniff, "why?"

"Where exactly in Germany?"

"I don't know," Nicky said ungraciously, "some place called Ham-something. Hamburg. No, Hamil. Something like that. In the north."

"It was Hamelin, wasn't it?"

"Yeah, I guess. Why?"

"Ever heard of the Pied Piper of Hamelin?"

213

CHAPTER 28

THE GROUP AROUND THE table gaped at Cat.

"The Pied Piper of Hamelin?" asked Nicky. "Come on, Cat, that's a fairy tale!"

"Well, maybe it is, and maybe it isn't," said Cat. "Up until a few months ago, neither of us would have believed in dimension travel and other worlds, would we? Yet here we are."

"Hmph. Fair enough," said Nicky, "but what does that have to do with you torturing me with mice?"

"I think you might be another part that was missing from our plan," said Cat, "and the answer is in here." She pulled a faded cloth-bound book from her market basket, which sat on the floor behind her chair. She turned to the Ruphians. "Just to get you up to speed, *The Pied Piper* is the story of a rat catcher who rid a town of a rat plague by luring the rodents with his flute and leading them into the river to drown, and when the town—it was called Hamelin—refused to pay his wages, he came back the next day and lured their children instead, led them with his pipe out of town and into a mountain, and they were never seen again."

"Oh," said Sepp, "*The Rat and Piper*! That's what we call that story here; remember, Guy, Mother told it to us once. It's a wonder we weren't frightened of musicians for weeks afterwards. But I never really took it to be true—well, I never thought about it, I guess. Are you saying that Nicky, or Nicky's family, has something to do with this?"

"I believe so," said Cat. "That's why I needed to see if it was true. Nicks, it's obvious your flute playing, your piping, is drawing the mice. That's why they come after you. And remember—think back——even back in our world, almost every time you'd play, a mouse would show up sooner or later!"

Nicky shuddered. "I guess you're right. But—it didn't always happen, not every time, or I would have never been able to learn the flute in the first place."

"I think powers like this are much stronger in Ruph than they were in our world, if they were even present at all. I certainly never had The Knowing then—"

"Well, you've always known stuff," Nicky said, sounding as if she was beginning to forgive Cat. "She can just pull info out of the back of her head," she told the others, "always has. Playing Trivial Pursuit with Cat is almost pointless; she always wins. *And* she can put the stuff she knows together so it makes sense—she can make connections, you know?"

"That was just from work," said Cat. "As a reference librarian you have to remember stuff."

"No," said Ouska, "there are often latent signs of a gift, even when the gift is not yet awakened. Perhaps in your world, all gifts lie dormant. So, Monica, your ancestors hail from the town that had the rat plague many centuries ago?"

"Not only that," replied Cat in Nicky's stead, "I seem to remember something you told me about your Grandma Bauer's maiden name. Wasn't it Pfeifer?"

"See," said Nicky, looking triumphantly around the circle of faces, "what'd I tell you? She knows stuff! I totally forgot about that. Yes, Pfeifer, that was her name; I saw it written once in an old book that used to belong to her. Okay, clue me in: what's so important about that?"

"Pfeifer means piper," said Cat simply.

Nicky looked at Cat for a few seconds; then her mouth dropped open. "Are you telling me that I'm descended from *the* Piper?"

"Yes, that's exactly what I'm telling you. Like I said, it's in this book. There are old stories in the Ruph library that I'm quite certain come from our world; and by old, I mean really, really old, from the early Middle Ages and before—nothing newer than about 1300 AD. The Pied Piper legend is from the late thirteenth century; it might be one of the newest ones we have here. And there are parts to it that have been forgotten in our world, but were brought here and have been preserved. In this version it says, sort of parenthetically, that the Piper had a fling with one of the girls in Hamelin, and that that was, in fact, the reason they refused to pay him—the mayor's son had an eye on her himself, and out of jealousy of the Piper he convinced his father and the town council to refuse his payment. And, well, I think that the offspring of that fling was one of your ancestors, Nicks. You've got the piper genes."

"Wow," said Nicky, "that's brilliant. I'm genetically programmed to attract rodents. Yee-hah." She looked like she was ready to burst into tears again.

Sepp rubbed a consoling hand on her back, then leaned forward and fixed his turquoise eyes on Cat. "You said Nicky was a missing part of our plan. What did you mean?"

Guy looked at Yldra and Lozyb. "Do you know of the plan?"

"Some of it," replied Yldra. "I know it involves running those strange rat men out of town because you feel they are a menace. Also, Mother thinks they have something to do with the mouse plague, and you're trying to deal with that, too." She looked at Cat for further elaboration.

"Yes. Whenever I have seen one of those men, the mice were not far behind. And always grey mice, not the little brown ones Guy tells me are normal here. So we might be able to kill two birds with one stone—or two rodents with one trap, as it were; we might be able to get rid of the mice and the rat men at the same time. We have an idea of what to do with them, but what we were missing was a way to get them into our trap. We considered using the boys for bait, but it's too dangerous." She gave a sidelong glance at Guy's apprentice, who had a slightly mulish expression on his face. "No, Andy. We've been through this. It's not safe. We can't have them getting at you. This, I think, is much better."

"I still don't get it," said Nicky, "what does my flute playing have to do with any of this? Do you think the rat guys will follow the mice? Oh, good grief"—she covered her face with her hands—"you want me to play the flute to get mice to come *on purpose*! I'm not even going to think about it, I won't, I won't, lalala..."

"No, I don't think the men follow the mice—I think the mice and the rat men go together, but if anything, the mice follow the men. No, there's something else; it's in here."

She reached into the basket again, and Guy grinned as she pulled out yet another book and riffled through its pages. "Bookwoman!" he hissed, and Cat made a face at him.

"Here," she said as she found the right page, "listen to this. It's that story of Chaelia again; Nikor found it for me. Okay, it's really archaic language, almost like reading Chaucer—I'll have to translate as I go.

"'In the year of the beginning of the Council the land lay to waste. The—the—mountain, I guess——the mountain's mouth split in twain,' (I suppose it was the opening of a cave), 'and from it came the Grey ones and the Black, both in one group. They came down to the valley and made their home there—therein. Young they were, and tender, and of their number there were one hundred and three tens. The valley they took, and when they grew, made it their own. The slaves they ruled, and in their tongue' (they spell it t-u-n-g-e, weird)—'in their tongue, they call themselves the Rat, which is, the Council.'

"And then it goes on from there," Cat continued, "telling the story of how they subdued the people that already lived in the land——they just call them the slaves—and how they had this big falling out between their two factions, the Grey and the Black, which pretty much have been at war ever since, and so on and so forth.

"The point is that, from what I can gather, we're looking at around the year 1300, by earth time, when all this happened. The Pied Piper story in Hamelin took place around 1284, I think. A hundred and thirty Hamelin kids went into the mountain with the Piper——that's what the legend says—and a hundred and thirty younglings, or children, came out of the mountain in Chaelia. They called themselves the Rat, that's German for Council. I think they were pretty much the replacement for the rats that the Piper got rid of and was not paid for. Oh, the other thing about the version of the Piper story you have here in Ruph versus the one we have in our world is that in this version, the Piper doesn't drown the rats in the river; he leads them into the mountain, just like he does with the kids afterwards. I think it's very likely that something happened in that mountain—the kids and the rats magically combined, or whatever. The Chaelia stories suggest that as time went by, the people that originally came out of the mountain became more and more rat-like——and there you have it, the Rats of Chaelia. What do you think?" she asked, turning to Ben and Andy, who had listened to all this without a word.

Andy looked at her from under his black brows. "Yes, Mistress," he now said hoarsely. "The masters rule. They are the Rat, they rule the land. The slaves are not as the masters; we are dark and brown and fit only for toil."

Guy gave a grunt. "Don't let me hear you say that again, boy," he said with a stern glance. "Fit only for toil, indeed!" Andy ducked his head, but there was a gleam in his black eyes that Cat was pleased to see. "So," Guy continued slowly, "what you are saying is that these 'Rat' people are in fact those rat folk we've been seeing here, and they've brought the mouse plague with them."

"And because they are 'Rat' people," Ouska took up his thought, "Monica's piping will draw not only the rodents, but the man-rats as well."

"Yes, exactly," said Cat. "I think Nicky's piping can be the very bait we need to get them into our trap. Mind you, I'm not altogether sure—but even the rest of our plan is rather speculative, too, isn't it? It might be worth a try."

"I don't think I can do it," said Nicky tremulously, "I just don't think I can stand it. Actually call mice to where I am, on purpose?" A shudder ran across her frame.

Sepp rubbed his hand in a circle on her back. "Think, dear—if you could get rid of Tyrone the rat face, keep him from ever going near Ben again—if *you* could do this... Think of what he did to Ben, to Ben's hands..."

Nicky looked up at him. Then her eyes narrowed and she pressed her lips together. "That *creep*!" she spat out. "Okay, okay—it freaks me out like nothing ever has in my life, but—God, I want to be rid of him!"

"Good girl," said Sepp proudly.

"Let's try it," said Cat, "right now. Play, and try to look at the mice when they come out. You can do this, Nicks."

"No!" cried Nicky, panicked, "not yet!"

Sepp gave her shoulder an encouraging squeeze. "I'll be here, dear. Right here by you," he said.

She gave him a wide-eyed look. "Maybe if you—well, you couldn't hold my hand, I need that for playing, but hold me somehow? I feel a bit braver with you there," she said. "And I think I need to stand on the chair again."

"Aunnicky be bave!" Bibby said. "Uncayepp help Aunnicky!"

Cat smiled at the little girl. "You know it," she said to her. "Go for it, Nicks. We're all here to fend off the beasts if they try to get to you."

Nicky climbed on the chair with a rueful grin. "I do feel kind of stupid standing up here like this," she said. Sepp picked up the recorder from the floor where it had lain since she threw it at the mice, and handed it to her.

"Not stupid," he said, smiling his lopsided smile up at her, "perfectly beautiful." He wrapped his arms around her waist.

She turned the recorder over in her hands. "Good thing it didn't break when I chucked it, poor thing," she said. "Well, here goes nothing!" She took a deep breath and put the instrument to her lips. A shaky little run up the scale, and down again. She ended on a squeaky note and took the flute from her lips.

"I can't!" she said with a sob in her voice. "I just can't do it!"

"Bubba help!" said Bibby imperiously.

"What?" They turned to the little girl.

"Bubba help Uncayepp help Aunnicky be bave!" she repeated.

"Well, the little one has something there;" said Ouska, surprised, "she may well be right!" She turned to Guy. "Try it, boy," she said.

"Me?" said Guy, "how?"

"Yes!" said Cat. "That's it! Your ability to reinforce, to strengthen others' gifts! It might be just what's needed to help Sepp boost Nicky's courage. Give it a shot!"

"Very well," he said with a raise of one eyebrow, levered himself to his feet, and moved around the table to stand behind his brother. He drew his brows down in a frown, thought for a moment, then laid his hands on his brother's shoulders. "Do it, little sister," he said, looking up at Nicky. Sepp took a firm hold of Nicky's waist; she drew a deep, shaky breath, then lifted the recorder, and blew a chirping trill.

Up the register the tune ran, another trill, and then segued into a lilting Renaissance dance melody.

Twitching mouse whiskers poked out from beneath the dresser. One after the other, mouse after mouse skittered across the floor and gathered around the chair. Nicky's eyes were wide, and her fingers trembled, but she piped, and looked at the mice, and piped some more.

Suddenly a pounce, loud squeaks, a hiss, and a meow. The mice scattered, Nicky's flute tune broke off abruptly, and there under her chair was Greyface the cat, crunching down on a most welcome snack.

"Kiki eat mousie!" explained Bibby laconically, and the tension in the room dissolved into laughter. Guy took his hands from his brother's shoulders, and Sepp lifted Nicky down from the chair and gave her a peck on the cheek.

"Well done, Karana," he said softly.

"Hmm?" Nicky said, looking up into his eyes. "I can't do it without you," she said seriously then, "without you, and Guy, I think. Thanks, bro." She smiled at Guy.

"So," said Yldra, "we have a plan, do we?"

"Yes," replied Cat, "we do. And I think I just came up with another small piece that was missing." She looked at the cat walking out of the room with the remainder of her kill, tail pointed straight in the air, the tip waving nonchalantly back and forth. "Oh, and where were we? Ah yes, having a birthday party. I'm sure you usually spend it plotting to rid your town of vermin and creepy guys, don't you, Yldra?"

"But of course," laughed Yldra, "every year! Anyone for more cider?"

CHAPTER 29

"**G**UY, DO STOP FIDGETING," Cat said. "I'm sure the boys are going to do fine."

The potter gave her a nervous smile.

"I'm just not sure if I should be in there, keeping an eye on them, or if it's better to do it this way and let them work on their own," he said.

"Isn't Sepp in there with Ben?"

"No, he's outside," said Guy. "He wasn't sure either, so we decided to just let them be. But it's driving me mad, it is."

Cat looked out the window and laughed.

"Sepp's looking not much better than you," she said. "He's pacing in circles around the yard." She pulled open the front door. "Come on, Sepp, get inside before you freeze your nose off."

Her brother-in-law stepped over the threshold, a frown on his face. "I just don't know if they're all right in there," he said. "What if that curse hasn't worn off? What if..."

"Oh, come off it, both of you!" said Cat. "You just want to see what they're doing!"

Guy gave a rueful grin. "Well, yes, there's that too."

"Then for crying out loud, go look!" Cat said. "Here, if you're scared to, I'll go first." She resolutely went over to the workshop door, gave a brief knock, then walked in. "Hi, boys! How's it coming?" she asked, a little more brightly than usual, then shook her head at herself when she realized she was showing off to the men, who were following hard on her heels.

Andy and Ben were bent over the work table, one on each end, so completely absorbed in what they were doing they were oblivious to their surroundings. Ben's side of the table was littered with reddish-brown wood shavings; Andy's was smeared with clay in a rather similar colour. Guy walked around the table to look over his apprentice's shoulder.

"Not bad!" he said with a raise of his eyebrows.

Andy jumped. As if in a residual reflex, his hand jerked at the little figure between his fingers in order to crush it, but then he caught himself. "Oh! Master Guy... sorry..."

"No, *I'm* sorry," said Guy, "I didn't mean to startle you. You didn't even notice us coming in, did you?"

The boy shook his head.

"May I look?" asked the potter. "Only if you don't mind, though."

Andy shrugged and held out his flat hand with the little sculpture on it.

"Well done," said Guy, "very well done indeed. Look," he said to his brother, "it's a perfect little cat!"

"I know," said Sepp, "just like Ben's! They're not quite finished in the details yet, though. Here, may I?" He held out a hand for Ben's carving and brought it over for the other two to see.

"Sweet!" said Cat, "they're exact mirror images again! But oh, look, Andy, yours is missing a leg, the poor thing. You must have squished it when Master Guy made you jump. Good thing it's clay, so you can put the leg back on." She held the little wooden cat, with its tail curled securely around its four paws, next to the soft clay sculpture to compare them.

A loud *"Meeow!"* came from the cottage, and the three-legged kitten hobbled through the door, Bibby in hot pursuit.

"Dzonny come back!" she cried, caught the kitten and scooped him into her arms. He struggled wildly.

"Let kitty go, Bibby, he doesn't want to be held," said Cat. Bibby only clutched the kitten tighter, but he fought free of little girl's stranglehold and dropped to the floor. Mewing loudly, he hopped over to the work table and tried to rear up to put his front paws on Andy's lap. But his single hind leg was not quite equal to the task, and he tumbled over. Unabashed, he started purring, then gave a few cursory licks at his tail, which had suddenly appeared in his field of vision.

"Oh dear!" said Cat, quickly moving the wooden cat away from the clay one, "they work even when they're not finished!" She gave the carved cat back to Ben. "You'd better fix the missing leg on yours," she said to Andy with a smile, "or all we're going to get is three-legged cats, which won't do us much good."

The boy gave her a slight smile back, reached for the lump of clay under the damp cloth, pinched off a small piece to amend the sculpture, and became completely absorbed in his work again.

"Come on, let's leave them to it," said Guy. "We're obviously in the way here."

_ℓℓ_

"There is one more thing," said Cat to Ouska a day or two later. "You know those dreams I told you about? Plus something the boys said. There was something about stones, blue stones. I think it's what those Rats use to travel between their world and others, like we did with Guy's bowls. Now, if I recall those dreams right, the Grey Rats are out of stones; they were saying something about 'only one left'. I didn't hear them much, just once or twice, but that was one of the things I remember. But the black one, he was going to go back, I'm sure of it, and take the boys along with him. He's got to have some of those things on him."

"Hmph, yes, he likely does," replied the older woman, pausing the motion of the pestle in the mortar in which she was crushing herbs to mix into ointment. "And if so, he might use them to go back to his country, even without the lads, and then try to come back for them later."

"So we need to get those things off the last rat guy?" asked Nicky, who was sitting at the table in Ouska's kitchen, stitching a Ruphian skirt for herself. "How're we goin' to pull that one off? I can see scaring them into running, maybe, but making 'em hand over their plane tickets? I dunno. We'd have to *really* freak 'em out."

Ouska gave her new niece-in-law a look. "You might have something there, Monica," she said. "We might be able to do just that. We could make them see things that aren't there."

"How?" Cat asked. "Oh—is there a potion, Aunt?"

"Just so," Ouska replied. "Do you recall the spikeberry bushes in the Arbour?"

"Spikeberry? I don't know that I... Wait! Do they have really nasty-looking spiny leaves and bright red berries? A couple of them right beside the Septimus Tree?"

"Yes, those are the very ones. The berries are potent medicine; their juice makes a most powerful potion to calm the mind and soothe agitated feelings."

"Well, we don't want to soothe those guys," said Cat, "quite the contrary, I'd have thought!"

"Oh yes, of course," said the wisewoman. "But the spikeberry juice soothes only at first and in small doses; if taken in too great a draught, it reverses, causes visions that horrify, and exaggerates what one sees to nightmare proportion. And then it causes forgetting, a loss of memory of what went before. That is why we very rarely use the juice—that, and the difficulty in gathering the berries. You are right in saying the shrubs look nasty, Catriona; the spines on those leaves are poisonous. One puncture from those spikes will have you ill for days, and as the berries are at the very base of the leaves, collecting the fruit is something we only do when we really need it."

"So, we're out of luck then?" said Cat. "The Arbour is covered in snow; I don't see how we could get at those berries, even if there are any left to gather."

"Fortunately, I have a small bottle of the juice I made two seasons ago," Ouska said. "Atyrra Paperseller was unusually bad that year with her fears and worries; a few drops of the juice in a cup of cider helped her much. But she got better before all the juice was used, so there is almost a full vial left. It does soothe at first, makes the person lose all their worries and be quite docile so they do as they are bid. But if one takes too much..."

"Oh!" said Cat, "I get it! We'll need the Septimus cups. There are three of those—no, four, I think. Let's see, how could we do this? We'll need everyone in on it..."

CHAPTER 30

F ROM HER VANTAGE POINT at the side of the market square, Cat looked across at Uncle's cider stall in front of Ruph's town inn. *This whole scene looks like it came straight off a Christmas card,* she thought as she pulled her cloak more closely around herself to guard against the chill. It had snowed again during the night, and the roofs of the inn, the town hall, and the library were covered in thick white feather blankets; the rose bush in front of the inn, bare of leaves now, was shrouded in a veil of snow. With his grizzled beard, round cheeks, and short nose, which the frost had painted a red nearly as deep as that of his heavy wool cloak, Uncle looked like Santa Claus personified. A cloud of steam rose from the cauldron he was boiling over a brazier, the fire in the metal basket crackling merrily. A few of Ruph's townsfolk were milling around the stall, and more were coming; the rumour of Sardor Brewmaster's new batch of mulled cider had made its way around the town in less than an hour. This was just what they had hoped for—they needed the rat men within hearing of the square for the plan to work. Cat squeezed

Bibby's little hand in hers and gave a sidelong glance down the narrow opening to Horseyard Lane, which ran between the corner of the hall and the library. In the shadows of the alley she could just make out the shapes of Andy and Ben, drawn up against the gate that led into the carriage yard behind the hall.

"Uncle's got the bottle?" she asked Ouska in an undertone.

"Yes," the wisewoman replied in the same voice, "it's in his pocket. I've told him the precise amount of cider to add the spikeberry juice to; one half jug should be about right."

Any time now, any time...

Uncle laughed at his friends and neighbours, all clamouring for a taste of his brew, and continued setting out cups on the table beside the brazier. He clapped his hands together, and Cat would not have been surprised to hear him break into a hearty 'Ho, ho, ho'. *All we need now to complete the scene*, she thought, *is some carollers*—and there they were. Nicky, Sepp and Guy, cloaked and booted, stepped out of the inn doors. Cat squinted across the square. The plan was beginning to roll.

Nicky, wearing the fingerless mittens Cat had knitted her just a couple of days ago, had her hands wrapped around the mouthpiece of the flute to keep it warm. Sepp put down the wooden box he carried behind Uncle's cider table. *Leave enough room,* Cat thought, *you need enough space to stand behind her!* As if he had heard her thought, Sepp picked up the box and moved it over, leaving a good four feet between it and the inn wall, wiggling it around in the snow to make sure it was firmly placed. Cat hoped the

231

box was tall enough; Nicky had to be able to keep playing without fear of the mice reaching her.

Her friend tested the balance of the box with her foot, then Sepp gave her a boost, and her blonde head suddenly appeared above those of the townsfolk at the cider stall. She looked clear across the square, and her eyes met Cat's. Cat looked over at Ouska, then down at Bibby. They were ready. Another look at Nicky, a nod, and a thumbs-up. Sepp stepped behind his wife and wrapped his arms around her waist. Guy stood beside them, laying his hands casually on his brother's shoulders as if in a gesture of affection. *They do make the most perfect tableau*, Cat thought to herself. She drew a deep breath to calm the hammering of her heart. *I just hope this works, please, please, let it work...*

Then Nicky raised the flute to her lips, and blew the first trill. One run up the scale, another one down, and half-way up again into the first few notes of 'The Lady by the River'. She drew out the notes, made them vibrate, sing. Cat got caught up in the beauty of her friend's music, which soared clearly out over the square. *It's working,* she thought, *the sound must carry over half the town!*

And then they had their proof. From between the houses, from under woodpiles and behind snow-covered planter boxes, small grey shapes emerged. They scurried along the frozen ground, not even looking for cover, drawn to the inn and the flute that was enticing them. The mice began to gather at the foot of Nicky's box, and Cat could see the frightened look in Nicky's eyes and heard the notes waver just a little. *Keep playing, Nicks, you can do this, you can do it!* she thought at her, *keep it up!* She saw both Sepp and Guy tighten their hold, and the tune became more confident. Nicky had gone to improvising, a haunting, lilting melody that brought images of green hills, clear mountain streams, towns, and villages into Cat's mind. Somewhere with the edge of her mind she noticed that the townsfolk at Uncle's stall had drawn back, stepped aside into the alley by the side of the inn, moving away from the ever-increasing stream of mice that were coming from every direction.

Nicky's tune became a call, luring, daring—and then Cat saw their real prey. Between the smithy and the cobbler's, from the western side of the village where the cheap tavern was, the grey rat men appeared. There were three, to Cat's surprise—Tyrone, the one Andy had called the slave master, and a third who looked vaguely familiar to Cat. Then she suddenly remembered: she had seen him on horseback in her dream. So he had found his companions? So much the better—they could be rid of all of them at once. Then from the other side of the square came—*Oh no!* thought Cat, *what is she doing here?* A giggling Kashinka stepped into the square on the arm of Mosrim the black rat man.

"How can we get rid of her?" Cat frantically whispered to Ouska. But the problem solved itself. Mosrim saw Nicky and a stunned look came into his eyes. He dropped Kashinka's arm, and all four rat men moved across the square towards the piping woman as if drawn by a magnet, oblivious to each other's presence.

233

"Hey!" called Kashinka, stopped dead in her tracks. Her face showed complete shock at being so suddenly abandoned, and her lower lip pushed out in a pout. "Hey!" she repeated, and with narrowed eyes watched the progress of the black-haired man towards her rival. Then with an angry toss of her head she flung her hair over her shoulder, spun on her heel and flounced out of the square.

"Wait for it," said Cat under her breath, "almost... here we go..."

And just as they had planned, Uncle stepped into the path of the rat men, cutting off their way towards Nicky.

"A draught of hot spiced cider, my good fellows?" Cat heard his voice booming out across the square. His large hands were spanned around the Septimus cups, pushing them at the men. *Thank goodness he is so quick-witted,* Cat thought. They had reckoned with three rat men, not four, but he had had another cup in reserve. The rat men pulled back, trying to side-step him.

Nicky's music changed, and the tune seemed vaguely familiar to Cat. What was it? Then the words began playing in Cat's head. "Eins, zwei, drei, vier, / lift your stein and drink your beer / Drink! Drink! Drink!" the flute insisted. *Brilliant, Nicks, brilliant!* thought Cat, and she watched as the rat men, as if under a compulsion, took the cups out of Uncle's hands and put them to their lips.

"Now?" she hissed at Ouska, but the wisewoman shook her head.

"Not yet! Give the spikeberry a little time to work," she whispered back.

Cat nodded. *Right, I knew that*, she thought, and took a firm hold of Bibby's hand.

The rat men across the square staggered just a little, and one after the other they sank down on the seats Uncle had so obligingly placed by the side of his stall. Their faces had taken on a glazed look, and they stared at Nicky piping her tune. Below her feet, the ground was seething with small grey mice, still more of them streaming from between the houses.

Right. Cat squared her shoulders. Part Two of the plan was about to come into action.

She looked across the square, catching Guy's and Sepp's eyes, and gave them a nod. This was the tricky bit—would Nicky be able to handle this? Apprehensive, she watched as Guy removed his hands from his brother's shoulders. Sepp seemed reluctant to let go of Nicky. *You can do it,* Cat thought at them, *you're strong enough for this!*

But then she watched in surprise as a change came over her friend. Still piping on, Nicky had a new expression on her face. No longer frightened, she looked directly at the mice milling about her feet, letting her gaze travel across the moving mass of rodents; in her eyes was a challenge, a masterful force. Suddenly she moved. Trilling some high notes with only the fingers of her left hand on the sound holes of the instrument, with her right she unclasped Sepp's arms from around her waist. She briefly looked down into his eyes, then using his raised hand as a support she stepped off her dais into the scurrying mass of mice on the ground. Her fingers went back to the flute, and its melody changed to a commanding marching tune. The mass of vermin parted to let her through and then surged back together to fall into a procession behind her.

Nicky piped and stepped ahead. *She's dancing!* thought Cat, astonished, *she's leading them in a dance!* Nicky walked past Uncle's table and out into the square, the mice scurrying after her in a stream of small grey bodies. She danced past the rat men on their seats, stepping lightly to the lilting and piping of her own flute, the mice streaming after her in a river that was now widening, now drawing in. The rat men half rose as if to follow her in the dance, their faces slack-jawed and their heads rolling just a little. The spikeberry juice was doing its work.

Guy stepped in front of them. Mosrim, the black rat man, fell back onto his seat.

"The stones, my man!" Guy commanded, holding out his hand in an imperious gesture. Cat saw the rat man mumble something and draw back, but he bumped into Sepp, who was standing hard behind him, his hands raised, ready to use force if needed. The rat man's eyes crossed slightly; then he visibly gave up his resistance. His hand went into the pouch at his waist and came back out with two small blue stones, their gleam winking across the square even in the falling dusk. He dropped them into Guy's waiting hand, looking up at the potter from under drooping eyelids with his mouth hanging open. The grey rat men beside him stood swaying, watching the stones with a look of slightly puzzled recognition, as if they knew they should do something to interfere, but couldn't pull themselves together enough to be bothered.

Guy's fingers closed tightly on the two small stones, and he took a step back. Sepp gave Mosrim a shove from behind, and the rat man staggered to his feet.

Nicky, piping steadily, danced in a circle around the square, the mice following behind in a seething, whirling stream. Again she danced past the rat men in front of the inn, and now they stepped out to her piping. With unsteady legs, they stumbled after her as she led men and mice across the square, towards the narrow opening of Horseyard Lane.

"Go now!" said Bibby, just as Cat was about to pull on her hand to lead her out and Ouska had placed a hand on her shoulder to tell her the same. Just ahead of Nicky, they ducked through the opening. Andy and Ben sprang from the sides of the lane, and, hands joined, the women, the boys, and the little girl ran through the gates into the carriage yard behind the hall.

They stopped in the middle of the yard. Andy and Ben threw back the hoods from their dark heads and faced each other. Cat reached for Bibby's and Ouska's hands, and they formed a ring around the boys, who drew from their pockets the figures they had made. They raised their hands, in one the carved and fired owls, in the other the clay and wooden cats, and held them at the ready.

Cat was facing the gate into the yard; at her back lay an opening in the wall, which led out towards the road to Ilim. Bibby on her right and Ouska on the left were also looking towards the gate, waiting. Only a few moments passed, the trilling of the pipe coming nearer and nearer, and then Nicky came dancing through the gate. The grey mice funnelled through the opening behind her, and the rat men stumbled into view. One, two, three—where was the fourth?

More mice poured in. Nicky began to circle the group in the centre of the yard, the rodents streaming after her—then Cat saw them: Guy, Sepp, and Uncle herding the last of the swarm of vermin and Mosrim the black rat man, staggering after Nicky's pipe.

Ouska and Bibby had seen, too. "Now!" the three cried together. The boys responded. A'verelm pushed his left hand, holding the owl, towards his brother's right and its mirror image figure; Br'oldyn's left hand, holding the small carved red cat, joined the identical clay image in his brother's hand. They laced their fingers and pushed their palms together.

An owl swooped overhead; a four-footed shape leapt up on the roof of the carriage shed on the side of the yard and hissed.

The mice circled; the rat men staggered after them. But where were the rest of the owls and the cats?

"It's not working," cried Ouska. "We need more!"

Suddenly Cat felt a hard punch, and she knew by the squeeze of Ouska's and Bibby's hands that they felt the force of the Knowing, too.

"Bubba!" "Guy!" they cried out together. "Come help!"

Guy understood immediately. He sprang from his place by the gate, where he had stopped and stood watching, darted between and through the seething stream of circling rodents, and reached the small knot in the middle of the carriage yard in a few great strides. He reached over his little girl's head into the circle, clapped his hands on the shoulders of the boys in its centre, and grasped them hard. His eyes squeezed shut, he dropped his head. Beads of sweat began to stand out on his forehead. Cat directed all her thoughts at him, trying to strengthen him, and she felt the same coming from his aunt and his small daughter.

The boys' hands began to vibrate. The Piper's tune trilled, commanded, shrieked, the rodents and rat men streamed around and around in a great, spinning maelstrom, circling the group in its centre.

Suddenly the boys' hands shook in a tremendous spasm. All at once the air was full of rushing wings, rustling feathers, great yellow eyes, and sharp curved beaks. A huge flock of owls swooped into the yard over their heads, their claws at the ready as they dived at the rodents.

The rat men screamed and ducked. Tyrone made as if to break away, back through the gate into the lane, but Sepp blocked his path, his fist drawn back ready to strike.

"No, Sepp!" Cat yelled, "don't! This way!"

Uncle jumped in to help. The rat men shied away from the older man's powerful stride, and Sepp and Uncle together drove them to the corner of the yard towards the opening to the road. The pipe's tune rose to a shrill cry.

"Again!" called Ouska, "hard!" The boys pushed their hands together, and another paroxysm went through them. As one, the great birds converged on the rat men. Desperate screams went up from their throats. They threw their arms over their heads to guard themselves against the razor-sharp talons, and they ran, clawing at each other in their haste to get through the gate and out onto the open road, away from the horror.

Nicky piped, and circled, in a wilder and wilder dance. But now, her flute piped up the scale, once, twice, and once more in a shriek, and abruptly she halted, the mass of grey mice coming to a halt with her.

Then Catriona saw that the roofs of the sheds around the yard were alive with cats.

"Kikis!" called out Bibby. The town cats of Ruph pounced.

—ell—

"There really aren't any of the grey mice left," said Sepp, cradling a cup of hot cider.

Cat looked at the myriad of tiny footprints on the churned-up ground in front of the inn.

"It sure looks that way," she said, "although I can't believe that the cats and the owls really cleaned them all up. There were way too many of them for even the Ruphian cats to get rid of. I think they must have gone as they came. Once the Rats were gone, the mice that escaped the wrath of the pussies just—well, disappeared. Don't you think so?" she asked Ouska.

The wisewoman took a sip of hot cider, some of the last bit that was left after Uncle had treated half the town to his brew—the brew without the spikeberry juice, of course. "I do believe you are right, child," she said. "We needed the cats and the owls to make a start, but once that was done, the vermin took themselves off."

"What finally happened to them," Nicky asked suddenly, "the rat guys? I didn't really see what went on, I was kind of busy."

"That you were, girl," said Uncle. "And you did very well, very well indeed." He nodded his head in the direction of the country road. "They ran. I've never seen anyone run so fast; some of the biggest owls were still after them far down by the bend to Adane's farm, where the road leads into the valley."

"They won't be back," said Ouska comfortably. "If the spikeberry worked the way I think, they'll run until they exhaust themselves, and after that, they will remember nothing but horrible nightmares of flying monsters. I don't believe they will even have a memory of why they came to Ruph in the first place, let alone want to ever return."

"Thank goodness," said Cat with a shudder. "They really gave me the creeps. The black-haired guy wasn't quite as bad as the others, by a very slim margin, but still..."

"Poor Kashinka," Sepp said with a lopsided smirk. "There goes another boyfriend." Nicky choked back a laugh, and Cat grinned at her. Suddenly she caught her breath. Right by Nicky's foot something moved—something twitchy and whiskered. Sepp followed her gaze, and both of them held their breath. *Please don't look down,* thought Cat at Nicky, *please don't!*

But Bibby sabotaged her. "Mousie!" she called, pointing.

Nicky looked. And calmly kept looking, as a small brown wood mouse softly scrabbled out from under her seat and looked up at her with its black button eyes, whiskers twitching.

"Hmm," said Nicky, gazing into the small creature's eyes, and she reached out a finger until it nearly touched the mouse's nose. "You're kind of a cute little thing, aren't you?"

CHAPTER 31

"WELL, I SUPPOSE THIS one'll do," said Nicky, perusing Cat's outfits, which were spread on the box bed. "The white blouse with the embroidery around the neckline, and the blue skirt. They're pretty much the dressiest thing you've got, not much more than the others, but at least a bit. Are you sure you don't mind me using the green top?"

"Of course I don't," Cat said. "Not that it's really fancy, either; I wish we both had something nicer to wear. I didn't even know how dressy they get with the feast until a couple of weeks ago. I guess we'll have to see about getting something nice to wear for next year. But the green blouse probably works better for you than for me, anyway; the sleeves are a little short on me."

"Yes. I just need to hem them up a tiny bit; then it'll be perfect," said Nicky, folding up the other few tops and skirts that they had decided against. "We can't always be dazzling everyone with high fashion. Did you see Sepp's outfit, though? He's got this gorgeous turquoise vest. It's going to strike sparks from his eyes."

"Oh, does he? They must have a matching set then, he and Guy. Really nice. Guy gave Andy his old vest, kind of a forest green one; we had to practically force the kid to accept it. I wonder if Sepp had one of the green ones, too? It would be neat if the boys could match. Where are they, anyway?"

"Out back, I think, stacking up the woodpile. Ben's starting to talk again. He used to be really chatty; it's been weird having him so quiet."

"Yes, I know," Cat said. "Remember, I heard some of the audio from when he was first with you. I think it's the adjustment, the shock of going from one world to another. He's not really sure who he is any more. But he's finding his feet, don't you think?" Cat put the last of the garments into the clothing chest and closed the heavy lid.

"Yeah, I think so," said Nicky, settling herself in the carved rocking chair. "It's a bit weird how he keeps flip-flopping between normal talk—well, okay, what's normal in our world for a kid his age—and sounding like something out of Shakespeare. About all he's missing is the *thees* and *thous*."

"I think that's the language of Chaelia," said Cat. "Andy never learned to speak any other way, so that's how he talks, and I think when Ben is with him, or is being Br'oldyn, as it were, when he remembers that aspect of himself, he falls into that way of talking. But he's not really comfortable with it yet, so he doesn't say much. Andy hasn't got that conflict; he just never talked at all until that curse got broken, and then he just went back to talking the way he was used to. I think Ben will figure it out——once they're here for a while, they'll probably start sounding like everyone else. Do you want a cuppa?" Cat hoisted the iron teakettle. "I think there's enough hot water left for both of us. Anyway, I'm glad Ben is getting a bit more cheerful again. It must be pretty strange for the boys to meet again after—what, ten years?"

"Nine, I think. He said he was five when they were separated, and according to the birth certificate I had for him, he's fourteen. Born on September 25th. But then, come to think of it, that might have been hogwash; they probably just made that up. But age fourteen fits, about, wouldn't you say?"

"Yes, it does; they're both at that voice-cracking all-arms-and-legs stage, and I think that's not unusual at fourteen," Cat said. "So Ben is going to apprentice to Sepp, is he? That's kind of funny, too, seeing as Sepp's never had any formal training himself. I suppose we could find another woodworker for Ben to work under, but..."

"Are you kidding me? Sepp wouldn't hear of it, he's not letting anyone else get their hands on Ben! No, he's going to teach him himself, and I have to say, it makes sense. I mean, Ben really likes him; I think he'd learn well from him. Besides, Sepp says that because I was Ben's guardian in our world, that means I'm responsible for him, and now that we're married, the responsibility is his share as well. Not sure if he's just making that up, though."

"No," said Cat thoughtfully, "that's how we ended up with Andy. They have odd ideas about teaching responsibilities here; the apprentice is bound to the master's family by contract. Andy started out sort of indentured to Kaltbur; he's their—well, I suppose *our*—brother-in-law. And when it didn't work out with Kaltbur, they shipped Andy off to Guy, which apparently still fulfils the contract. So it sounds about right that if Ben is 'bound' to you, as they'd say here, your husband fulfils some of that obligation by teaching him a trade."

"You know, I wouldn't want to let him go now, anyway," said Nicky, "I've gotten darned fond of that kid."

"As we have of Andy," said Cat. "Bibby would have a thousand fits if he left. It'll be hard enough on her having the boys live at your place, once you get your new house ready with that extra bedroom for the boys, and only having Andy here during the day. But I have to say, I'm thankful—we just haven't got the room for two extra growing bodies around here. Two *big* growing bodies," she smiled, and laid a hand on her stomach, "there's enough for a tiny one, though."

"That's right," said Nicky, put her hand over Cat's and bent down to address Cat's belly. "Do you hear that, baby? You do lots of growing, and get big and strong for Aunty Nicky! I can't wait to meet my first nephew. Actually, wait, no," she straightened up, "he won't be the first; Ben's my nephew. And Bibby's my niece. They're proliferatin' quite amazingly."

"Speaking of Bibby," said Cat with a look out the window, "there she is. Look, aren't they cute?"

Nicky followed her gaze out the window to see Guy and Sepp stepping along the forest path, each of them holding one of the little girl's hands. "One, two, fwee, whee!" Cat could hear Bibby's voice through the window as the little

246

girl was lifting up her legs, wanting to be swung up by her arms. Laughing, the men obliged, and with a few more swings the little girl was deposited in front of the door of the cottage which Cat had pulled open to welcome them.

"Bubba bwinged pwesents! An' Uncayepp bwinged pwesents for Aunnicky! Bubba and Uncayepp bwinged pwesents fwom..."

"Shush, you little magpie!" Sepp interjected, scooping up the little girl under one arm and clapping his hand over her mouth. "Don't ruin the surprise!"

"Wooin supwise?" the muffled little voice came from behind his hand, and he laughed.

"Just give it to them already, will you," he said to his brother, "I don't think Bibby and I can hold out much longer!"

Guy pulled a large cloth-wrapped bundle from the pouch slung over his shoulder and held it out to Cat. "It's not purple or silk..." he said with a twinkle in his turquoise eyes, "but maybe you'll like it anyway. There's one for little sister, too."

"Guy! What did you do?" Cat untied the string that was wrapped around the parcel and pulled back the fabric covering. She gasped. Soft folds of the deepest sapphire blue lay in front of them.

"Wow!" said Nicky, reaching out to lift up one of the garments. "This is gorgeous! Where did you get it?"

"The dressmaker's—Yldra helped with the choosing and the sizes," said Guy, and the brothers watched with identical lopsided smiles as their wives shook out two brilliantly blue ankle-length gowns, sleeveless in the style of a surcoat, with turquoise-ribboned lacing down the sides, the necklines and armholes embroidered in the same shade of Septimus blue as their husbands' vests. Underneath the gowns lay two white underdresses in simple linen, the long sleeves straight and tapering to a button at the wrist.

Nicky held the gown against herself, swayed back and forth as if she was dancing, and gave Sepp a glowing look. "Darlin', you've really done it this time!" she said. "Oh, but—out, out, out!" She shooed the men towards the workshop. "Go wait in there and make sure the boys don't walk in on us! We need to try these on!"

"Mumma Aunnicky dwess!" said Bibby, with round eyes.

"Yes, sweetie, and you can stay here while we're changing, you're a girl," said Nicky, picking up the undergowns. "Oh!" she called out suddenly, "look!" Beneath the white chemises lay another, smaller garment, blue like the overdresses. "Is this what I think it is? Look, Bibby!" She picked it up and shook out the folds.

The little girl squealed. "Bibby dwess, Bibby dwess!" She danced from foot to foot with excitement, holding out her pudgy hands for the little gown.

The men laughed and retreated into the workshop.

CHAPTER 32

T HE EARLY DUSK WAS falling at the end of the short
solstice day as Cat stepped out of the library. Behind
her, Nikor Archivist was locking the big double doors.
It had only taken about half an hour to get him to put
aside the tome he had got lost in (one of the more obscure
volumes of dragon lore), convince him that it was indeed
winter solstice day and the feast would be starting soon,
help him find his slightly moth-eaten feast vest (black vel-
vet, embroidered in gold thread), and persuade him to run
a comb through his fringe of silver hair to render him
respectable-looking for the celebration. "Yes yes, feast day,
feast day," he muttered, as he turned the heavy brass key
in the lock and slipped it into the pocket of his vest. The
left-hand chest pocket, it was; Cat made a mental note
of it, because she was certain he would forget which and
then stand in front of the locked door afterwards looking
bewildered.

Cat picked up the long skirt of her feast gown and
made her way across the market square, where her family
was gathered in front of the town hall. *My family!* she

thought, amazed. *I have a husband, a daughter, a brother, a sister, two nephews... I have a home!* Joy trickled through her and then settled in her stomach in a curious mixture of pleasure, anticipation, and—well, butterflies. The whole town of Ruph was gathered here today, with more feast participants arriving by the minute, streaming across the market and entering through the great carved door into the hall. With each opening of the doors a blend of warm light, buzzing voices, clinking crockery, and delectable smells spilled out onto the snow of the marketplace, to be cut off again when the heavy doors swung shut, until the next visitor, hard on the heels of the last, pulled the doors open once more. In the centre of the market a great stack of fuel was piled up, well-seasoned wood built into a ten-foot-high teepee, ready for the solstice bonfire that would usher in the new year at midnight.

This almost feels like convocation, thought Cat. *I'm actually nervous about walking in there in front of everybody!* She smiled at Ouska's neighbour, who had come with her family, the children chattering excitedly, and gave a little wave to Chelm, who clapped his brothers on the shoulders in passing as he made his way into the hall. *Not just a brother and sister,* Cat thought, *lots of them. Brothers, sisters, uncles, aunts, cousins, nephews, nieces... Like Guy said, half the town is related to us. To us. I'm part of this town...*

Guy, Sepp, Nicky, and the boys with Bibby were waiting for Cat just a little to the side of the hall doors. Sepp bent down to whisper something in Nicky's ear, and she laughed up into his face. Cat had never seen her friend looking so happy, and a smile of pure pleasure spread over her own face in response. Then she caught Guy's eye. He was watching her progress across the market square, the look of pride and admiration in his eyes making them shine with an almost physical light. He stepped forward to meet her, holding out his hand.

"May I lead the most beautiful woman in town to the feast?" he asked, half teasing, half serious, taking her hand in his and making a leg.

"No, you may not," said his brother behind his shoulder, "that's my job!" and he drew Nicky's hand through his arm.

Guy laughed. "Let's not quarrel about it, just for today," he said. "Are we ready?"

Bibby, holding Andy's hand, was dancing with impatience. "Go feas, Mumma, go feas!" she cried excitedly. She looked adorable in her little ankle-length gown. The blue-green embroidery, which matched the ribbon threaded through her red-gold curls, echoed the colour of her father's and uncle's vests; it made their turquoise eyes sparkle brilliantly. *The Septimus blue*, Cat thought; *it's my favourite colour!*

Her eyes went to Nicky, who was looking nothing short of delectable, the sapphire of her gown shimmering in the light of the torches that were burning beside the hall doors. The lacing of the gown, pulled tight to fit just right, moulded the dress to Nicky's curves; her curls were a riot of gold, held back with a ribbon in a blue just one shade deeper than the gown. But for the first time in their friendship, Cat felt not one twinge of envy at her friend's beauty and undeniable sense of style. The memory of the look in

Guy's eyes when he had first seen Cat in her own sapphire gown brought a slight blush to her face even now.

"Go feas!" called Bibby again, tugging on Andy's hand. The boys wore matching vests as well—as Cat had thought, Sepp had had a vest to give to Ben, dark green like Guy's old one, which was now Andy's. Bibby reached out and took hold of Ben with her other hand.

"Come," said Guy, and led Cat forwards. Sepp, holding Nicky's hand, stepped in behind them, and the boys with Bibby between them brought up the rear. The townspeople streaming towards the hall doors suddenly stopped and fell back to form two lines, leaving a path clear between for their little procession. Guy reached out for the large iron loop of the door handle. *Here we go!* Cat thought and drew in a deep breath to steady her nerves.

The warmth and brightness of the hall flooded over her. Long trestle tables ran down the length of the building, laden with bowls, platters, jugs, and pots that gave off deliciously scented steam and were heaped with delicacies sparkling jewel-bright in the light of the myriad of candles shining from wall sconces and the candelabras standing on every table. More than half of the benches running along the trestle tables were already occupied with Ruphians in their feast finery in all colours of the rainbow, and an excited hum of conversation filled the hall.

Suddenly a buzz went through the crowd. "The Septimissimus!" they whispered, then called, "The Septimus brothers! The Shapers and the Septimi!" It seemed to Cat that every eye turned to them; then all of Ruph was on its feet, and a shout went up from the crowd that shook the rafters. Cat gave a sidelong glance at Guy, gripped his hand more tightly, then threw a look back over her shoulder at Nicky, as wide-eyed as herself. Like Sepp, Guy had drawn himself up, his head held high, and with a look of immense pride the Septimus brothers led their wives down the length of the hall, to the cheering of the people of Ruph. They reached a place close to the head of the centre table, where a spot had been reserved for them among the members of the Septimus clan, and when Cat encountered Yldra's wide smile she realized that her own face held a smile just as wide and as proud, and a thrill ran through her, right down to her toes.

Guy helped her climb over the bench and take a seat beside Ouska and Uncle, across from Yldra's family, her brothers, and other Septimus cousins. Guy and Sepp had their hands shaken and their backs slapped by the men, their brothers first among them. Yokan, whose family sat just a few places further down the table, roared with laughter when his back slap made Sepp's eyes nearly start from their sockets; his wife Inga, a round-faced cheerful woman, leaned across the table to press Nicky's and Cat's hands, almost upsetting a jug of steaming spiced cider in the process. A red-gold-headed Septimus girl, Inga's daughter, gave an interested look at the twins, who were taking their places between Cat, Guy, Nicky, and Sepp. There was a great scraping of bench legs and rustling and chattering as the feastgoers settled themselves back on the benches, and more and more came into the hall to fill the remaining empty spaces.

Finally the eldest elder, a bent and wizened little woman with snow-white hair who had her place at the head of the table on the farthest right, declared the feast open, and everyone fell to with gusto. They ate, they drank, they talked and laughed and ate yet more, and when Cat felt she could not fit one morsel more (but ate one more stuffed plum, all the same), everyone vacated the benches, and with surprising efficiency the tables were cleared, the boards taken off the trestles and stored against the walls, the benches ranged around the perimeter of the hall, and a large space in the middle opened up for dancing. Cat saw a group of ten or twelve musicians set themselves up at the head of the hall, tuning their rebecs, ouds, and dulcimers, and giving some experimental taps and jingles to hand drums and tambourines.

Guy and Sepp, who had been lugging tables and benches with the other men, returned to their wives just in time for the music to strike up.

"Madam Wife," said Guy with a lopsided eye-crinkling grin, holding out his hands to Cat, "will you dance with me?"

"With pleasure, Sir Husband," replied Cat in the same tone, and let herself be pulled to her feet. "Except I don't know those dances," she said with a twinge of panic.

"They look really easy," said Nicky over her shoulder, as Sepp was leading her onto the dance floor, "either circle dances, or you just move to the music, right, darlin'?" she asked her husband. "They can't be too complicated if everyone's doing them. Look, even the little kids are in there."

Bibby was holding onto Andy's hand and bouncing up and down. "Bibby Andy dance!" she said, and with his little smile that was just for her he allowed himself to be tugged out into the middle of the floor.

The red-headed Septimus girl, egged on with much giggling by her sisters and cousins, dropped a curtsy in front of Ben, who had sat back onto the bench, tired after carrying tables. He turned rather red, although he did not look exactly displeased, and was about to shake his head when Nicky turned back, took his hand, and pulled him to his feet.

"C'mon," she said, "just pretend y'all are at a school dance!" He chewed his underlip, gave a sidelong glance at the girl, and muttered something about never having gone to those, but Nicky just laughed. "Then it's time you started, ain't it!" she said, and gave him a little shove in the girl's direction. "What's your name, honey?" she asked her.

"Nygelis Fishmansdaughter," the girl replied with a giggle.

"There you go," said Nicky, "Nygelis, meet Ben; Ben, Nygelis. Now off you go!"

Ben gave his little shoulder shrug and grinned shyly at the girl. As the music struck up just then, the two started bobbing to the beat of the hand drums and tambourines.

Guy led Cat into one of the open circles that had formed all over the floor and whirled her into the dance. Nicky was right, these dances were easy. They seemed to involve moving in a group in an open ring, with the first couple in the line setting the steps, and everyone else simply following what they were doing. Some groups were doing more complicated steps than others, and you could choose your group according to your preference for easy or fancy footwork. "This is like Greek dancing," Nicky shouted at Cat as they spun past each other. "Any second now someone's going to shout '*Opa!*'" Cat laughed as Guy swung her into a twirl, following the head dancers' leads, and his turquoise eyes twinkled down into her brown ones.

"Happy, Madam Wife?" he asked.

"So happy!" she replied, and he spun her into his arms and broke away from the dance. For a few moments, they were alone on the dance floor, swaying in a circle all by themselves.

"I love you, Catriona," Guy said.

"And I love you, Dyniselm Septimissimus," said Cat, smiling all her happiness up at him.

"Hey! Get a room!" Nicky hissed, grinning at Cat from just behind her.

Cat grinned back in sheer delight. "Same to you!" she hissed back, noting that Sepp and Nicky were stepping to the music in just the same intimate embrace in the middle of the milling dance crowd.

The music played on; new players took their turns at the instruments so the musicians could have a dance with their wives, husbands or sweethearts; the Ruphians danced, they rested, they refreshed themselves with draughts of cider and spiced ale, they danced some more; then all stood quietly while Sulyss Builderswife and Kaltas, her son, sang the ballad of 'The Wanderer Lost in the Plains', the boy's clear soprano blending with his mother's mellow, resonant alto in a sound whose sweetness sent shivers down

Cat's spine. Atyrra Paperseller, who was a poet, recited a brand-new narrative, and Cat was astonished to find herself, and Guy, and Sepp and Nicky and even little Bibby, but most of all Andy and Ben, cast as the heroes of the story of 'The Mice of Ruph', telling of the terrible rodent plague that lasted until the Shapers and the Septimi cast out the vermin and brought security back to the town. Yldra's brothers Charn and Chonyk then performed a stick dance together with their three apprentices, strapping young men muscular from their work in the fields in the valley outside of Ruph. Their staffs struck together, pulled apart with a clank, they jumped, stamped, leapt over the sticks, and struck them together again, and everyone clapped the rhythm to their dance, broke into a great cheer when it was finished, and swung back into their circle dances to the cheerful tunes of the rebecs and ouds.

So the feast went on far into the night. Little children fell asleep in their parents' arms or were bedded down wrapped in a cloak on one of the benches; and if they woke and cried, someone, anyone, rocked them back to sleep to the melody of the music.

And when Cat was just beginning to feel that she was ready for it to be finished, when her yawns became wider and ever closer together, the music came to an end. Her brother-in-law, Chelm Metalwright, the eldest Septimus son, stepped up, lifted a shining brass horn, and blew seven clear notes, four times in succession—'*seven for the sons of the Septimus, four for the seasons of the year*', Guy's words from another day echoed in Cat's memory. The eldest elder, who had been dozing in a corner for the last hour, shuffled to the front of the hall.

"The year is gone," she declared in a thin, wavering voice, "the Septimissimus will see it out, will name the old, and will lead in the new!"

A cheer went up from the crowd, and Guy once again drew himself up proudly. He took Cat's hand in his. Sepp, holding a sleeping Bibby in his arms, stepped into position behind him, Nicky next to him, Andy and Ben alongside. Two Ruphians threw open the big double doors of the hall, and Guy led Cat, Sepp, Nicky, the boys and all the people of Ruph out of the hall. He paused in the doorway and pulled one of the still-burning torches from its holder on the door frame, and then turned to the wood stack in the centre of the marketplace.

He waited until the town of Ruph had ranged itself, in a wide circle, around the square.

Then, standing tall, he grasped the torch with both hands, and raised it high above his head.

"The year is gone!" he called in a clear voice, "a year of pain, a year of pleasure! A year of sorrow, a year of joy! The year is gone. I call this year," he paused, and Cat felt the anticipation of the crowd, waiting for the naming, "I call this year—the Year of the Mouse!" And with this, he thrust the torch deep into the wood stack. Some pitch inside the stack caught the flame, and instantly the fire flared up.

"The old year is gone," shouted Guy over the crackling of the flame. "We welcome the new!"

A tremendous cheer went up from the people ranged around the square. They shouted, clapped, and stamped for what must have been a full five minutes, as the flame flared higher and higher until the whole stack of wood was alight in a huge bonfire.

Then Guy turned around and reached out for Cat. He took her hands in his and looked deeply into her eyes. "Catriona Potterswife, this has been the best year of my life," he said quietly.

"And mine," she said, looking up at him with a smile that radiated her love.

He bent and kissed her right in front of the whole town of Ruph.

"Speaking of the Year of the Mouse," said Sepp, who was still holding Bibby, "there's one more thing I have to do." He passed the sleeping little girl over to her father.

Then he turned to Nicky, reached into the pocket of his vest, and pulled out a little leather pouch.

"Monica Outlander," he said, "no, Piper. Monica Piper, my wife, this is yours."

Nicky looked, her eyes big in her face, as he opened the pouch and let a silver necklace slide out into his palm.

"I love you, Monica Piper," said Sepp.

"And I love you, Sepp—Risyl? I love you, Risyl Woodwright!" said Nicky.

Sepp picked up the silver wedding chain and clasped it around Nicky's throat.

The pendant was a mouse.

NOTE

While spikeberry bushes and the potion created from them only exist in Ruph, the other plants and recipes in this story work in Cat and Nicky's old world, as well. Mint, thyme and camomile are supposed to be good for a headache (although they don't work as quickly when they're not taken in a Septimus cup). Boiling black walnut husks in a rusty pot, or a regular pot with some rusty nails, stinks quite badly, but the result is a great semi-waterproof ink that lends itself well to writing or drawing with a dip pen. Ouska's sourdough bread can also be reproduced in a modern kitchen, if one has time, patience, and the willingness to do some hard kneading.

Acknowledgements

A shout-out to all those who helped make this book happen:

Peter and Anna, without whom it would not exist—my alpha-readers, cheering squad, suggesters of plot ideas and necessary changes, suppliers of hugs, tech support, moral support, mental health support, etc.—

My friends, beta readers and fellow writers Lee Strauss, Christopher Bunn and Desi Valentine, whose feedback was invaluable—

My editor of the first edition, Jennifer Ballinger, whose expert editing helped me learn the ropes—

My critique partner, editor, and most of all *friend*, Louise Bates, who was part of the whole process of the first *and* the updated edition—

And all my readers who enjoyed Seventh Son and said they couldn't wait for the sequel—

I couldn't have done it without you.

THANK YOU!!

About the Author

Angelika M. Offenwanger lives in rural Western Canada with her family, two cats, numerous dust bunnies, and a small stuffed bear named Steve. She has been known to make sourdough bread, and black walnut ink from the nuts in her garden. Online she can be found on Facebook and Instagram @amoffenwanger, and on her website at www.amoffenwanger.com.

www.ingramcontent.com/pod-product-compliance
Lightning Source LLC
Chambersburg PA
CBHW031708170626
46808CB00005B/1654

* 9 7 8 0 9 8 8 0 4 1 2 5 7 *